Brotherly Love

Wings Press, Inc.

Mike Axsom

Brotherly Love

Romo reached in the back of the van behind the driver's seat and pulled out a roll of duct tape. "What are you going to do with that, Romo?"

"I'm just going to pull off a couple small strips and tack it on the back of the seat here. In case he starts hollering like a little girl, I'm going to put the tape over his mouth, then I'm going to handcuff him. Just hope nothing goes wrong."

"It's about five minutes until seven. You better get ready," Hammy warned.

Romo got out and opened the sliding door, leaving it open as he got back in. "Okay, I'm set. By the way, if things go wrong, I want you to go back to the hotel, clean out your room, and get the hell back to North Carolina as fast as you can. I've fixed it so there is no evidence of you ever being here. Everything is in my name."

"Nothing is going to go wrong, big guy. You just throw his ass in the back. I'll take care of the rest." Hammy reached in his back pocket and pulled out a plug of Red Man. Rather than taking his pocket knife and cutting off a piece of it, he just stuck in his mouth, bit off a big mouthful, and slid it all to one side of his jaw.

"Now, don't forget to push the sliding door button once we get in. I sure would hate to be going down the road and fall out of the van. Wouldn't that be a hell of a sight?" Romo said.

Looking in his rearview mirror, Hammy yelled, "Here he comes, Romo. It's showtime!"

The black Mercedes pulled up in front of them and stopped near the curb. "Okay, get ready."

"I'm ready. Let's do it."

Hammy started the van. Once the bodyguard opened the door to go into Starbucks, Hammy pulled up beside the Mercedes. Romo jumped out and opened the back door of the Mercedes. Zanetti leaned over in the seat with a terrified look on his face. Romo grabbed Zanetti by his suit jacket and jerked him out. He took one step toward the van and threw him through the open door.

Brotherly Love

Mike Axsom

A Wings ePress, Inc.
Mystery/Crime Novel

Wings ePress, Inc.

Edited by: Jeanne Smith
Copy Edited by:Christie Kraemer
Executive Editor: Jeanne Smith
Cover Artist: Trisha FitzGerald-Jung

All rights reserved

Wings ePress Books

Acknowledgments

I would like to thank Molly Williams of Mayodan, North Carolina for preparing this book to be submitted to a publisher. You did a great job Molly. Thank you very much for all your hard work.

I would also like to thank my two daughters, Heather Wilson and Malia Barrett for their assistance in editing recommendations and their support throughout this novel. I love you both.

Also, I would like to thank my two sons-in-law, Brad Wilson and Rudy Barrett for their continued support and for keeping my laptop and my webpage in working order and up to date. Thank you both for all your hard work.

Thanks to my good friend Lynn Chandler Willis, the author of *The Rising* and *Tell Me No Lies*, for giving me ideas on how to continue this book. Love ya.

To my brothers JB Axsom, Roger Axsom, my sister Linda Corns, and my nephew Keith Axsom, thank you for all your suggestions and continued support. I love you guys.

Dedication

To my grandchildren: Avery Wilson, Sydney Wilson, and the
one to be in November.
Love you all, Papa.

One

Paul stepped from the plane terminal, a suitcase in his right hand, and a carry-on bag over his left shoulder. He stood out from all the other passengers who were exiting the flight...someone you would look at twice. Weighing about one hundred and eighty pounds, and six feet tall, he held his shoulders back, walked very erectly, and projected a military attitude that demanded respect. Dressed in casual, stylish attire, he had neatly combed black hair that was sprinkled with gray on the sides.

Romo had seen that exact walk many times when they were together in the boys' home. Memories came rushing back. When they were at the school, he had respected Paul so much for the way he had taken care of him. Romo was smaller than most of the other boys; however, he was never bullied, because everyone knew Paul was his big brother. If anybody picked on Romo, he had Paul to deal with, and nobody wanted that.

The last time Romo had seen Paul was at his mom's and dad's funeral two years earlier. Romo's wife, Mary, had passed eighteen months prior, so Paul knew Romo was alone. Paul stayed four days with him then, before he went back to his home in Philadelphia. Now, Paul was back again to attend Romo's retirement dinner. Paul would be the only family member there for the celebration. It seemed as though his big brother was always there when he needed him the most.

Romo stepped out in the middle of the passengers as they rushed to gather their luggage. Paul saw him right away. A big smile came across his face as he set down his luggage and rushed toward Romo with outstretched arms, wrapping them in a bear hug.

"How are you, big brother?" Romo asked as they walked shoulder to shoulder down the corridor.

"I'm doing fine, Mo, now that I'm here. I hate flying on those damn airplanes."

Understanding his dislike of flying, Romo replied, "I know that's not your favorite thing, but I'm so glad to see you. Thank you for coming to share this special occasion with me."

"Well, you know it had to be special for me to get on an airplane!"

Changing the subject, Romo asked, "How is that nephew of mine, Tyler, getting along?"

"He's doing fine. I asked him to come with me, but he had to work, plus, I don't think his new wife would have liked that very much. I think she likes to keep him close by."

"And Maria, how is she?"

"Well, that's something we'll talk about over a drink when we get to your place."

"Uh-oh. That doesn't sound too good."

"Oh, yes, it is," Paul replied with a grin.

As they arrived at Romo's car, he opened the back door and put Paul's luggage inside.

"What are you driving here, Mo?" Paul asked.

"Mom and Dad's car. When they passed away, I sold mine and started driving theirs."

"Well, there's nothing like a Mercedes, you know."

"Yeah, you knew my parents. They always liked the best."

"There's nothing wrong with that."

After about a twenty-five minute drive, Romo pulled up in the circular drive of his home, which backed up to the Greensboro Country Club. It had been built back in the late thirties or early forties; a two-story white brick with six white columns on the front. An upstairs balcony went all the way across the front of the house. The lower front porch was patterned like the balcony with white spiral picks matching the bottom and top banisters.

Admiring the impressive house, Paul exclaimed, "Man, this is a nice place. It looks bigger this time than it did before. What's the square footage?"

"I think it's around five to six thousand. I'm not sure. I loved growing up in this house with Mom and Dad and Ms. Blackstock. This is where Dad taught me how to play golf. I had a great childhood here."

"It makes me feel good to hear you say that. You deserved it."

"Since I grew up in this house and loved living here, it just made sense to move back. With Mary gone, our house didn't feel the same anymore. There were too many heartbreaking memories, so I just decided to sell it. Now, there's nobody but me and Ms. Blackstock."

"So she's still here?"

"Oh, yes, she'll be here until the end."

"I knew Mr. and Ms. Lindy thought the world of her."

"She's definitely like family, and she still takes care of me just the way she did when I was a little boy. She continues to correct me today just as she always has. And I don't question her, either."

Paul laughed out loud. "Well, somebody had to keep you in line. Mr. and Mrs. Lindy let you do whatever you wanted."

"You're right. She's one of a kind."

Romo looked at his watch. It was three-thirty and getting about time to go inside, fix a drink, relax, and catch up on each other's lives. When Romo opened the front door, there stood Ms. Blackstock with her arms wide open. Paul put his arms around her and with warmth in his voice, he asked, "How have you been, young lady?"

Flattered by his charm, she answered. "I've been good, Paul. I'm so glad you came for this event. You need to come see us more often."

"I know I do, Ms. Blackstock, but they keep me pretty busy at the police department. I would like to see my baby brother more often, though."

"Oh, yes, he is a baby all right."

"Have you had to tan his hide lately, Ms. Blackstock?"

"Not lately. But he knows I'll give it to him if he needs it." Everyone laughed at her remark.

"Go on into the library, Paul. We can fix a drink in there, and then go out and sit on the patio."

As Paul walked into the library, he was in awe. The first thing he noticed was the beautiful oriental carpet woven with deep maroons, dark blues, and rich tan colors that showed excellent taste and beauty, yet felt very comfortable. The furniture was oxblood-colored leather consisting of a sofa and two wing back chairs. On one wall a huge rock fireplace rose from the floor to the ten-foot ceiling. Shelves tightly packed with books lined another wall. Like the enormous fireplace, the shelves extended from the floor to the ceiling. They were made of solid cherry and were so shiny they appeared to be covered with glass.

As Romo walked over to the built-in bar near the fireplace, he asked Paul what he preferred to drink. "Jack and Coke will be fine. Mo, I'm totally impressed with this room. It's beautiful and interesting. It appears Mr. and Mrs. Lindy did a lot of reading."

"Dad did. He did a lot of research for NASA, and when we weren't playing golf, he was in here reading about the moon and stars and the atmosphere. You may not know this, but he had a degree from Harvard; he earned a doctorate in physics. He was a smart gentleman, but he was easy-going and always down to earth with everyone. I loved that about him."

About that time, Ms. Blackstock stepped into the room. "Y'all go on out on the patio. I'll bring you some snacks shortly," she announced.

Romo and Paul ventured out through the French doors onto the rock-covered patio. All around them were beautiful live plants, neatly arranged, and some in bloom. Out over the golf course, and just beyond the lake, stood a white colonial clubhouse. The view was lovely as well as relaxing.

In the center of the patio was a round table covered with pieces of multi-colored stained glass. Four bamboo wicker chairs and a sofa made of bamboo offered seating space and coordinated with two small end tables covered with the same stained glass.

Paul commented, "This is certainly a peaceful area."

"Mom and Dad would have coffee here most mornings, and now, this is where Ms. Blackstock and I drink our coffee. She's the one who maintains all these flowers. Have a seat."

"A lot has been going on that I need to tell you about," Paul said. "I know you've been very busy, and so have I. We haven't had much time to talk, so I'll give you an update. Some of it is good, and some of it's not so good."

Romo took a sip of his drink. He could see the serious look on Paul's face and wondered what he was about to hear.

Sensing this, Paul admitted, "I know you don't know any of this, so I'm going to start from the beginning. Maria and I have been divorced over two years. It just got to where she and I couldn't talk sensibly to each other at all. In fact, it got so bad, I stayed gone as much as I could. When I was around the house, there was nothing but an argument. She obviously felt the tension because she started staying away from the house more herself.

"As you know, Tyler was in college. He was in the middle of his third year, and all a sudden he came to me and said, 'Dad, I want to quit college and join the Philadelphia Police Department.' I knew he was dating some young lady who worked as a legal assistant for a couple of attorneys downtown, and I could tell he was very much in love. After he graduated from the Academy, I managed to help get him a job in communications at the department. At least that would keep him off the street and in a nice office at the precinct. Shortly after that, he and Sarah got married. I helped with the down payment on their house, they moved in, and they both seemed to be really happy."

He took a sip of his drink, moved a coaster in front of him and set the glass down. Taking a deep breath, he continued. "Then I got to thinking, why am I here putting up with this crap? Tyler is married, and out on his own. I just don't need this shit anymore. So I found a townhouse. It was a nice two-bedroom across town in a quiet neighborhood, so

I moved the hell out, and filed separation papers. Sometime after that, Maria started dating a motorcycle cop by the name of Eddie Reynolds. We had known him and his wife, and when Eddie's wife died, Maria started dating him. As far as I know, he seems to be a good guy and a good cop. They got married about a year ago and all I can say is, God help him."

Romo laughed at Paul's wry sense of humor. Paul took another sip of his drink and laughed along with him. Without hesitation, Romo asked, "Are you happy with your life now?"

"Yes. I'm very happy. I'm at peace with myself, and I'm enjoying my new job."

Two

“What is your new job, Paul?”

“Well, I accepted a job in the Internal Affairs division.”

“Internal Affairs? That doesn’t sound like you.”

“I know. I thought about it for about a month, and then the colonel came to me. We had a long talk. He told me they needed me because there were things going on in the police department he didn’t like. He said he needed a good honest man to go in and find out what was happening. The colonel hesitated for a few minutes, not sure just how to begin, and then he began to tell me of his concerns.

“Someway, somehow, items had started going missing from our evidence room. It happened numerous times right before a trial would begin. Then the judge would throw out the case due to lack of evidence. We had to find out about this missing evidence. We felt confident it had something to do with the mob in Philly. Most of the stuff that was missing involved mob members. They were always being acquitted due to lack of evidence."

"Gosh, Paul. You've got your hands full. You're facing a pretty stressful situation, it sounds to me."

"That's not the half of it. The main problem I have is Tyler," Paul explained. Surprised, Romo asked, "What's Tyler got to do with it?"

"Part of Tyler's responsibility is keeping inventory and maintaining items in the confiscation room. I would like to think he's not involved in this, but it's awkward working around him and having these thoughts running through my head. You know I'm going to do my job and do it right to the utmost of my ability, so you can see what I'm up against. I'll just have to let the pieces fall where they may."

"Is there anything I can do to help?"

"You already have by letting me get this off my chest and knowing that what we say stays between us. I'll find out what's going on. It may not turn out the way I want it to, but I will get to the bottom of this. The good thing about it is that the colonel and I are the only ones who know about it. I guess you could say that right now I'm working on my own."

"Well, just know I'm here for you if you need me."

"I know, Mo. Having your trust means a lot to me. You don't know how much I appreciate it." As they were finishing their conversation, Ms. Blackstock walked through the door with a tray.

"Here you go, boys, grilled cheese sandwiches, potato chips, and peanuts. This should hold you over until dinner."

Romo thanked her and turned to Paul. "Are you ready for another drink?"

"Maybe one more. What time do we need to be at your retirement dinner?"

"It starts at eight. We should get there around seven-thirty, so we'll leave here around seven."

Paul looked at his watch. "Well, it's five now. We'll just have one more, and then we should probably start getting ready."

"Sounds good to me," Romo replied as he picked up Paul's glass and went into the kitchen for a refill.

When he came back, Paul asked, "What do you plan on doing after you retire?"

"Well, I'm going to play more golf, and I've signed up for shagging dancing lessons."

With a quizzical expression, Paul asked, "What the hell are shagging lessons?"

"It's a dance that started at Myrtle Beach, South Carolina, back in the late 50s and 60s. They play all that good music by The Drifters, The Coasters, Al Green, and all of the oldies you and I grew up with. Mary liked to dance. She always told me I had rhythm, and she thought I could dance if I tried. So, I'm going to start taking shagging lessons."

"So you'll just play more golf and take dancing lessons?"

"I'm sure I'll be finding other things to do along the way. Are you planning on retiring anytime soon?"

Paul took a sip of his drink and slowly put it back down on the table. "You know, Mo, I have never given it any thought. I enjoy being a police officer. Now that I'm living alone, and Tyler is out on his own and with Mom and Dad gone, there's nobody I feel responsible for. I think I'm going to continue working until I've had enough, and I don't know when that's going to be."

"Well, now that I'm retiring, I can come up and spend more time with you."

"I'd like that. It's been a long time since we spent some quality time together."

"Yep, and I'm going to make up for it. Maybe we can go over and visit our old school again."

"That would be nice. I go over about once a week and check in with the folks. In a way, it still seems like home to me."

Realizing the time, Romo said, "We'd better start getting ready. We have about an hour before show time."

"I can be ready," Paul said as he took the last bite of his grilled cheese sandwich. "Man, that was one good sandwich!"

"If you think that was good, just wait until she serves breakfast in the morning."

"I can't remember the last time I had a home-cooked breakfast."

"Well, you're going to have one in the morning, Paul," Ms. Blackstock said as she stood in the doorway with her white apron on and both hands on her hips.

Romo turned around to Paul. "Come on and let me show you the guest bedroom and bath. Make yourself right at home, and I'll meet you on the patio within the hour."

Forty-five minutes later, Paul, wearing a dark blue suit and a red necktie, met Romo on the patio as planned. Admiring him, Romo commented, "You dress up pretty good, buddy. I really like that suit."

"Thanks. I have plenty of sport coats I wear to work, but since this is a special occasion, I decided to wear this suit."

"I have a couple of suits and, hopefully, one day, I might be able to get back into them." Looking down at himself with his arms spread out, Romo explained that his gray pants and navy blue sport coat would have to be suitable for the occasion.

"You look fine. You're right in style. I'm ready to go if you are."

Three

Romo pulled out of the drive and headed up Elm Street to the Shriners Club on High Point Road where the party was being held. After getting through town, Paul looked over at him and said, "This is a personal question, Mo, but I was just wondering if you're dating anyone special now."

Romo was a little surprised with the question. "I don't know if you'd call it dating, but I've been out to dinner with a few lady friends and I feel guilty as hell doing it."

Paul was silent for about a minute after listening to Romo's confession. "Well, Mo, I hope what I'm about to say doesn't offend you, but I am your brother, and your well-being is my concern. You shouldn't feel guilty. I'm sure Mary would have wanted you to move on with your life. I don't think she would have wanted you to live the rest your life alone. I know it's difficult, but you've got to keep going, buddy."

"I know, but it sure is hard. She's on my mind constantly."

"I'm not saying to forget her. That will never happen, I know. I think getting involved in things you enjoy will help divert your attention."

"You're probably right. I'm going to start implementing your advice immediately. Thanks, friend, for your kind words." As Romo pulled into the Shriners Club, the parking lot was full and he had difficulty finding a place to park. "Wow, I wasn't expecting this many people."

"Obviously you made some kind of impression, or this many people wouldn't be here."

"I can't imagine what kind of impression I would have made. Maybe these folks just didn't have any other place to go, and we do have a free open bar tonight."

"That's it, Mo. They're just here for the free drinks," Paul said with a grin.

As they walked in the front door, two policemen in uniform took them through the double doors leading into the banquet room. About 200 people stood and started applauding. Paul was shown to an empty chair in front of the stage. Romo was led up on stage and seated in a chair beside the podium. When the applause subsided, everyone took their seats. This was not what Romo had been expecting. With an embarrassed look, he glanced down at Paul who gave him a smile and a thumbs up.

Then, Major Clarence Chumley stepped onto the stage and walked over to Romo. He shook his hand warmly, and commented, "This is not what you were expecting, is it, Romo?"

"Not at all, sir."

Chumley, a tall slender man in his mid-fifties, dressed in neatly pressed full uniform, stepped to the podium.

"Good evening, ladies and gentlemen. Please continue enjoying your dinner. We're here to celebrate the retirement of one of our own homicide detectives, Romo Lindy. His brother, Paul Riggs is also a homicide detective, with the Philadelphia Police Department, and is here with us tonight. Stand up, Paul. We're glad you could make it. A brother of Romo's is definitely a friend of ours. Thank you for coming."

Glancing at his notes, the major continued with background information about the honoree.

"Romo attended Wake Forest University and studied law for five years. Seven months before graduating with a law degree, he joined the Navy and trained as a Seal, graduating at the top of his class. While spending five years in the Navy, he was sent on several missions the Navy would not disclose. He then resigned from the service and joined the FBI. Romo completed his training and became a training officer in self-defense. He also served in various secret missions.

"After eleven years with the Greensboro Police Department, and his service with the Navy and the FBI employment, he is able to retire at forty-one years of age. After attending several schools with Romo and having the opportunity to spend some social time with him, I can truly say I have not met a person with more integrity and honesty. He says what he means, and means what he says. He is a true gentleman, and I am pleased to say Romo Lindy is my friend. Obviously, many of you feel the same way."

The audience stood and applauded.

Chumley continued, "Now, I'd like to recognize one of Romo's fellow officers who has already retired, but spent a year as Romo's partner in the homicide division. He would like to say a few words. Come on up, Hammy Lee."

Hammy walked up on the stage and stepped in front of the microphone. Romo noticed that Hammy had gained weight since his retirement, so much so that he couldn't button up his sport coat. That sure didn't matter to Romo, however, because Hammy was not only a prior partner but a really good friend.

Hammy addressed the crowd. "Most everybody out there knows I'm not a public speaker. I am definitely not good at this, but because of my friend, I've agreed to speak. And believe you me, that's a pretty big sacrifice." There was low laughter from the crowd.

"Romo and I worked side by side for about a year and, after working with somebody for a year, you really get to know that person. We drank coffee together, ate lunch together, rode in a car together for eight and nine hours, and participated in day-long stakeouts together. The things that occurred while he and I were on duty, and the things we got involved in...there was no doubt, he had my back and I had his.

"Of all the things he and I have been through, there was one particular night that will stand out in my memory forever. It was about three in the morning, and we received a call that there was a fire on Spring Garden Street. We were nearby, so I turned the car in that direction to see if we could be of assistance. We pulled up in front of a house where a crowd had already gathered in the yard. We got out of the car just about the time the fire truck pulled up. There was a woman in pajamas standing in the crowd screaming, 'My baby is in there! My baby is in there!' Romo was standing beside me, and all of a sudden he was gone. I started looking around for him and then I looked toward the house. He had taken off his coat and was pulling his tie off as he was turning on the outside faucet and hosing himself down.

"About that time, I saw a fireman enter the house in full gear. As Romo walked up on the small porch on the side of the house, he pulled his coat up over his head, took his necktie, and tied it around his head like a bandana to hold the coat in place. He opened the side door where smoke was billowing out, got down on his knees and went inside. I was pacing back and forth like a first-time father at the hospital. I kept my eyes on the front door. I know he was only in there three to four minutes, but to me it seemed a lot longer than that. About that time, the right side of the roof caved in. I just knew he was a goner. People started shouting, and the woman was still screaming, 'My baby, my baby!' The firemen started moving the crowd back to the road.

"I had to show them my badge to be able to stay close to the house. I'm watching the front door, and all of a sudden, I see this big dark shadow coming through the open front door. Romo was dragging something with his right hand. As I moved a little closer, I could see it was the fireman who still had all his gear on. It looked like something you would see in the movies. I ran up on the porch. Romo handed me a rolled up blanket. I took it, and then I realized it wasn't just a rolled-up blanket. There was a baby inside. I walked down the steps into the yard and reached down and unfolded the blanket. There was this little baby with big dark eyes looking at me. He actually grinned at me. The mother was there in an instant and grabbed her child. I turned to look for Romo. He had the fireman under his arms and was dragging him off the porch. We had no more gotten him out in the yard when the whole house caved in. I grabbed Romo by the arm and turned him around. 'Are you okay, Mo?'

"I couldn't believe the first thing that came out of his mouth. 'Yeah, I'm fine. I'm just wet as hell, that's all.' He said it as if it were no big deal. After the fireman and the mother with the baby were put inside the EMS vehicle, I said, 'Mo, you saved their lives.'

"And he said, 'I don't know about that. I just happened to get to them first.'

Hammy paused and looked over at Romo, who was sitting there quietly, looking down at the floor. Hammy was thinking how Romo wouldn't take credit for a good deed. *He acts like it embarrasses him when people say good things about him.*

"But I'm here tonight to tell you that he was one hell of a police officer, and I was proud to work with him. I wanted this story to be told. He will never tell it, so I'm here to do it for him."

Again, everyone stood and applauded.

Hammy walked over to Romo, who stood, shook Hammy's hand and sat back down, shaking his head slightly as Hammy walked off the stage.

The curtains opened behind Romo and a Navy officer, with his hat tucked under his left arm, walked toward the podium. He turned toward Romo, who stood and addressed him at attention. The naval officer saluted and Romo, keeping his composure, saluted back. The officer adjusted the microphone to fit his height.

"Good evening. My name is Major John Appleton. I am a Navy Seal with Unit Six. I served with Romo Lindy for four years. He and I went through basic training at the same time. And yes, we went on some missions I'm not able to discuss here tonight. I am going to discuss, however, a certain instance that happened while we were on duty together. I cannot give you the details of that project itself, but I'm going to tell you what happened while on this assignment. On this particular mission, there were eight of us. We were not allowed to carry any firearms. The only weapon each of us had was a knife.

"Our submarine surfaced just enough that all eight of us, in scuba diving equipment, could slide off the side. In total darkness, we started our mission. It took about an hour to get to the beach. Upon arrival, we took off our scuba gear and hid it among the rocks. Each Seal was responsible for his own location in order to retrieve his gear at departure. After a successful mission, we were to head back through the marshland to recover our equipment and then swim back to the submarine. The sun was just beginning to come up and its reflection was coming off the water in our direction. We had to be back in that submarine before daylight. Time was running out. We had to move fast.

"We were about one hundred yards from the beach when all of a sudden, a siren went off in the direction we had just left. Strobe lights came on. We lay down and started crawling on our stomachs as the strobe kept moving back and forth over us. When we approached the edge of the beach, we started gathering our scuba gear, putting everything on as quickly as possible as we scrambled toward the water. A bullet struck my air tank and entered my side. It damaged a nerve in my back, causing me to go down. I had no feeling in my legs, and my air tank had lost all its capabilities. I knew I was a goner. It would be just a matter of time before I would be captured.

"All of a sudden, I felt two hands grab me from behind and start taking off my diving gear. It was Mo. He yelled frantically, 'Come on, Johnny. We've got to get the hell out of here!'

"I can't walk, Mo. My legs are dead," I told him.

"About that time bullets were firing all around us. Mo yelled, 'We can't stay here, Johnny.'

"The next thing I knew, he was dragging me out to sea, bullets still singing by us, as we got into deeper water. The tide was coming in, which made it more difficult to swim, but with the waves coming in higher, it also gave us cover out of sight of rifle fire for about twenty more minutes. Romo was swimming with one arm and holding me with the other. I was doing my best, moving my arms to give him as much assistance as I could. All the other divers were underwater headed toward the submarine. About halfway there, it had gotten lighter, and we knew the submarine was not going to come up in daylight. Time was of the essence.

"All of a sudden, Romo looked at me and said in a calm voice, 'Hold on, buddy. We got company.' I looked around, and sure enough, there were some fairly good-sized sharks swimming around us. Then I realized I was bleeding from my side, and my blood was drawing them. I knew we had fought a good battle, but the more I bled, the closer the sharks started coming in to investigate. I told Mo to get the hell out of there because they would stay with us as long as I was bleeding.

"'Can't do that, buddy. We're in this battle together.' One particular shark started getting closer and closer. Mo looked at me and said, 'Stay still. Don't move any more than you have to, just enough to stay afloat.'

"That shark looked to be about seven to eight feet long. He swam right up next to Mo, and when he did, I could not believe what happened. The next thing I knew, Mo had sailed on top of him with his knife in his right hand, and they both went out of sight underwater. I was looking around waiting for them to resurface. Everything was eerily quiet. I just knew that shark had taken Mo down to the bottom. I had accepted the fact that Mo was gone. It was just a matter of time for me.

"About that time, a sound like the top of a volcano exploding interrupted the silence. Water went in every direction and right in the center of the explosion, that shark went straight up in the air, twisting and turning, with Romo on its back. Romo's left hand was wrapped around the shark's head, gripping the inside of its gills, his legs wrapped around its body in a locked position. He drove the knife he was holding into the stomach of the monstrous fish, blood flying everywhere. The shark went back down under the water with Romo on its back. In just a few seconds, although it seemed a lot longer, Romo's head popped out of the water. He swam over to me, and I will never forget what he said. 'Come on, buddy. We got to get to that sub. They'll be serving breakfast in about an hour, and I'm getting hungry.' Needless to say, I was still in shock at what I had just witnessed, yet I felt calm. I knew he was confident in getting us back to the sub. He grabbed me again, and we started swimming. As I looked back, I could see the sharks that were around us before were after the shark that was bleeding profusely."

Appleton held up a little black square box. He took the lid off and in it was a Bronze Star, the symbol of bravery and valor in the line of duty. "When this medal had been presented to Romo Lindy at the time, he had declined to accept the medal," said Appleton. "Romo had said, 'I do appreciate the recognition, and that you would honor me with the Bronze Star. I am refusing this medal because I just did what I was trained to do, and that is to take care of the wounded and be sure everyone returned from the mission. I did nothing more than any of the other six men would have done if they had been in the same circumstances. So, thank you for the recognition, and that's enough for me.'"

Now, holding the Bronze Star in his right hand, the major said, "The only problem with what Mo said," as he slowly looked over at Romo with a grin, "is I don't remember going through training where we were shown how to climb on a shark's back and do what he did. You can't find that in the training manual, and I don't know how many men could have or would have done it; probably nobody but him. So when I heard about his retirement, there was no way I wasn't going to be here to thank him again for saving my life."

Appleton walked over to Romo and said, "You may not have wanted to accept this from the Navy Seals, but will you accept it from me, a husband and a father of two with thanks to you?"

Romo stood at attention. The major pinned the medal on the lapel of his sport coat and saluted him. Romo saluted back, and then they embraced. The major whispered his thanks again and Romo acknowledged his words with a nod. When the major walked offstage, there was a standing ovation. Romo sat back down, looking a little embarrassed.

There were three more speakers from the floor who told short stories of things that had gone on in the office concerning Romo. One mentioned that there was always light humor about Romo looking so much like Tom Selleck. The ladies called him Tom as they passed him in the hallway.

Romo looked up and saw Paul coming toward the stage. He stepped up to the podium, adjusted the microphone, looked over at Romo and smiled. "Now, you didn't know I was going to do this, did you, Mo?" Romo just shook his head, wondering what Paul was going to say. It was quiet as Paul began to speak.

"I am Romo's brother, Paul. I'm a homicide detective in Philadelphia. I came here tonight to celebrate my younger brother's retirement." Paul paused, feeling a little emotional, and then continued to speak.

"As the major was talking about Romo and the secret mission, I couldn't help but look around at some of your faces. You look surprised and shocked, but I wasn't. To me, this is what Romo does. He doesn't panic. He reacts calmly to the situation at hand. I think Romo realizes that if you panic, you lose control and can't think of what to do in an emergency situation. That is a rare talent. There are very few people who have that ability, and I know Romo has it. Romo is a true believer in right and wrong. He and I both have always said that if you're getting ready to engage in something, and if you have to think whether it is right or wrong, you can rest assured it is wrong. Romo believes in doing the right thing. I can stand up here for the next hour and praise my little brother but, as you can see, it's embarrassing him. So I won't continue to give him praise, but what I will say, and continue saying, is that I have always been proud of him and am pleased that I can call him my brother."

Romo got up and met Paul halfway. They embraced and turned to the audience with a slight bow of their heads as if it had been a stage play. Paul stepped aside. Romo took the microphone in hand.

"I would like to thank everyone for being here tonight. I am humbled by the attendance. I certainly was not expecting this many people. I would also like to thank all the speakers for their kind words. I will have to say that I had forgotten about some of those things that were discussed, although they have brought back a lot of good memories. Thank you very much, folks, for all your support. As a fellow police officer, it has been a pleasure serving with all of you." He laid his hand on Paul's shoulder and said, "And a special thanks to my brother Paul for coming down to Greensboro to share this event with me. As long as I can remember, he's always been by my side. I have always admired, respected and looked up to him, and always wanted to be the man he expected me to be. So with that, I'll say good night, have a safe trip home, and thank you for coming."

Romo and Paul had a few drinks and a quick dinner. Then they stayed for the next forty-five minutes shaking hands and saying goodbyes to all his friends.

The two men pulled out of the parking lot and headed for home. Both enjoyed a few quiet moments reflecting on the evening's activities. Breaking the silence, Paul looked over at Romo and said, "I've got to ask you this question, Mo."

"Okay, what's that?"

"What in the hell were you thinking when you climbed on a shark's back?"

Romo started laughing.

Paul said, "The way the major told it, I could actually see it happening."

"He may have dramatized it a little bit. I don't exactly remember it that way, but if he said that was the way it happened, I guess it did. I knew the blood was causing the sharks to come in close, and I knew I had to give them more blood to go after, so when the shark came close enough, I just reacted accordingly."

Paul sat quietly and looked out the window. Then he turned to Romo and said, "The only thing I can say is, that must have been one hell of a ride." They both got a big kick out of Paul's comment and laughed.

After getting home, they made themselves a drink and walked out onto the patio. Romo didn't turn on the patio light because the full moon was shining brightly. The only sound was the chirping of crickets in the distance. They both sat enjoying the night sounds and the gentle light breeze. Romo had questions he wanted to ask Paul and, after a few moments of relaxing, he thought it would be a good time to bring them up. Since Paul was about three years older, there were things he hoped his brother would discuss with him about his parents. He remembered asking the question when he was little, but Paul would never talk about it. All he would say was, they were good parents and they loved you, then he would change the subject. Remembering what Paul had said before, Romo decided he did not want to talk about anything Paul was not comfortable with. They were enjoying themselves in the quiet of the night, and Romo didn't want to spoil the mood.

"It was really a pleasure sharing your retirement celebration with you, being able to meet your friends, and hear all the nice comments they said about you," said Paul. "It's gratifying to know you've made very close friends who are going to stand by you in the future. It just reassures me that when I go back, I'll know you have enough support from your friends that you'll never feel alone. That makes me happy."

Romo sat for few minutes looking across the table at Paul's dark silhouette and didn't say a word.

Paul raised his glass. "Here's to you, little brother." Their glasses clinked in the quiet night air and they finished their drinks. "It's bedtime for me, Romo."

"Yeah, me too. Ms. Blackstock said she'll have breakfast ready at six. Goodnight."

~ * ~

The next morning when Paul went into the kitchen, Romo was already seated at the table. Ms. Blackstock had prepared scrambled eggs, country ham, red eye gravy, sliced homegrown tomatoes, and a bowl of grits. She was holding a wicker basket of biscuits she had just taken out of the oven. Paul sat and, as he pulled his chair up to the table, Romo reached over to grab a biscuit. Ms. Blackstock slapped the back of his hand. He jerked his hand back quickly as if he had stuck it in hot coals. Looking over at Paul, he gave him a wink."

"Now, just try that again, young man," Ms. Blackstock chided. "Now, you know we've got to say the blessing first, Mo."

"Yes ma'am. I know," Romo said with a big grin as he looked at Paul.

Ms. Blackstock sat and said the blessing. "Okay, boys. Ya'll can go at it, now."

After consuming breakfast until he felt the seams on his trousers would burst, Paul said, "Well, Ms. Blackstock. I may die on that airplane today, but I can tell you one thing. I will go down saying I've just eaten the finest meal I have ever had. Thank you very much."

"You're more than welcome, Paul. I just wish you would make plans to come see us more often."

"Yes," Paul replied. "I would love to do that." He then reminded Mo, "I believe it's about time we left."

On the way to the airport, Mo asked, "When you get back to Philly, what's the first thing you're going to do?"

"We're going to have to find another location to start storing all our confiscated goods. And we have to set up a security system to make sure everybody is checked in and out properly. That's got to be one of the first things. Then I'm going to start with the Mafia boys down at the waterfront and see where it takes me. I'm confident there is a connection there with the police department."

"Now that I'm retired, do you think I need to come up and maybe give you a hand?"

"No, it's going to be fine. It's just going to take a lot of time, probably day and night."

"It looks like you have about forty-five minutes before boarding. Maybe we'll have time for a drink before you take off."

Romo pulled into a parking space. In the airport, they stepped into the first bar they came to. Paul ordered a coffee but couldn't seem to hide his nervousness. "It's going to be okay, Paul. Nowadays, flying is like riding a bus," Romo said.

Paul replied quickly, "Yes, but I can step out of a bus if it crashes." He continued, "I'm glad to hear you say you've started back playing golf and taking dance lessons. That's a good thing but I would feel better if you had a lady by your side as you do all those things."

"I will. The right one will come along one day, and I'll know it when it happens."

About that time, an announcement came over the speaker that Flight 331 was getting ready to board to Philadelphia. Paul stood, picked up his suitcase and, looking deeply into Romo's eyes, said, "Romo, I can't tell you what's going to happen in Philly, but whatever happens, just know I'm your big brother and I will always be there for you." Then he reached up and lightly patted Romo on the side of his face. "Know your brother loves ya." Then he turned and walked toward the boarding gate.

As Romo was driving back home, he could not help but think of Paul's parting comments. It was almost as if he were saying goodbye. He thought about the sad look in Paul's eyes and how his voice was filled with such passion and sincerity.

Four

Five months had passed since Romo retired from the Greensboro Police Department. He was meeting three other retired police officers at a local golf course, Crooked Tree, which was about ten miles north of Greensboro. It was early Saturday morning on a warm August day, and it was going to be a good day for golf. He was getting ready to tee up on the first hole. He placed the ball on the tee and gripped the driver in his hand. Looking down the fairway, he admired the nice course, the pretty weather, and enjoyed being with close friends when his cell phone rang. His phone was in the cup holder in his golf cart, so he decided to let it ring, and check it later.

"Go ahead and answer it, Mo. You're not going to be able to hit that ball until you find out who's calling you. We'll wait for you," one of his friends told him.

He picked up the phone hastily. Not too happy about his golf game being interrupted, he answered with a somewhat cool tone of voice. "Hello, Tyler. This is a surprise. How are you this morning?" He listened and made no comment for a couple of minutes, then he said, "I'm going home and pack a few things, Tyler. When I get to the airport, I'll call and give you the time of my arrival. See you when I get there."

The other players could see that Romo was upset. They walked over to the golf cart and asked if he was okay. Romo looked up at them with sadness and despair on his face. He answered, "That was my nephew. My brother has been murdered."

Knowing his brother was a Philadelphia police officer, one of them asked, "Was he on duty?"

"I don't know, fellows. I've got to go catch a plane. See you guys later."

~ * ~

When Romo arrived at the Philadelphia airport and stepped off the plane, Tyler was waiting. Although Tyler had not seen him in two or three years, he recognized his Uncle Romo right away, as he stood out in a crowd. Tyler guessed him to be about six foot four inches and weighing about two hundred and forty pounds. He had short, black hair and a neatly trimmed mustache.

As Romo entered the airplane terminal, he spotted Tyler, and could see that he had grown into a fine looking young man who resembled Paul at his age. As they embraced, they both started to weep. They held each other for a few minutes, and then silently made their way to the car.

Tyler was the first to speak. "You're going to stay with me and Sarah, Uncle Romo. We have a spare bedroom."

"That's fine, Tyler. After you get out of this traffic, I want you to start from the beginning and tell me everything you know. Then I want your personal opinion as to what you think happened."

Tyler waited a few moments, and then began his narrative. "I'm sure Dad told you all about his and mom's separation, and her getting married to a motorcycle cop."

"Yes, he told me all about that."

"Dad moved into a townhouse in west Philly. He seemed to be okay with the split. At that time, I was in my third year in college, and Dad said the only reason he stayed with her as long as he did was because of me. He said that now that I was grown, in college and, basically, on my own, he could care less what she did or who she married.

"Dad had just gotten promoted to the Internal Affairs Division about the time he got back from Greensboro visiting you. Every time I would go over to visit him, he was working on something he wouldn't discuss with me. I was on the police force myself, following in his footsteps, so I was a little disappointed that he wouldn't tell me anything. I felt like he didn't trust me, but he would just say he didn't want to get me involved, and the less I knew the better off I'd be. Dad had a lot of friends in the police department. He was fair and honest and everybody knew that. That's why they respected him so much. He had a partner for a couple of months. Dan Robinson, I believe, was his name. Dan had to take a leave of absence because his wife contracted Parkinson's disease, and he had to stay home and care for her. So, Dad was working alone.

"After I arrived at work Thursday morning, I heard the dispatcher ask a patrol car to go by Fourteen Twenty-one English Street and check the residence. Dad hadn't shown up for work and that was unusual for him. He was always there about an hour before anyone else arrived on that shift. About thirty minutes later, all hell broke loose. Police cars were leaving the station with their sirens on, and everybody was talking on their radios about going to the address that I knew was Dad's.

"I started to leave my desk to see what was going on when the lieutenant walked up and put his arm around my shoulders. He said he needed to talk to me and, at that moment, I knew something bad had happened to Dad. They wouldn't let me go over there, but I did go to the hospital where he was taken."

Tyler hesitated for a moment, cleared his throat, and took a deep breath. "They said someone had broken into Dad's townhouse sometime during the night and shot him in the back of the head. Well, needless to say, Uncle Romo, I went all to pieces. All I've been doing is walking in circles for the last four days, and then it dawned on me, I needed to call you. I'm sorry I waited so long. I had so much on my mind I couldn't think. I found your phone number in Dad's wallet, and I called as soon as I could. He was cremated yesterday, and Sarah was going by to pick up his ashes on her way home today from work. She is a paralegal downtown. She'll be home in about an hour. We're having a police service tomorrow morning at ten at St. Joseph's Church and we're expecting a big crowd. I would like you to be with me, Uncle Romo, if you will."

"I'd be glad to, son."

"Well, here we are," Tyler said as he pulled into a cement driveway in a middle class subdivision. The house looked small and had a single car garage. The grass and shrubs were cut neatly, but so were all the rest that sat in a row in front of the houses in this Philadelphia suburb. As they walked in, Romo was impressed by the décor, very casual with the appearance of very expensive furnishings.

"Would you like a drink, Uncle Romo?"

"That would be fine."

As Tyler was preparing their drinks, Sarah walked in with some dry-cleaning draped across her arm. "Hey. How are you guys?" She walked up and stopped in front of their visitor. "This must be Uncle Romo," she said.

Romo stood as Tyler introduced Sarah. She replied with a smile, "So nice to meet you, Uncle Romo. Let me put these clothes away, and I'll be right back." Romo was impressed with her and her appearance. She was small, attractive, with blonde hair, and wearing a stylish red dress.

Tyler placed the drink on the bar, and Romo took a sip. "Now, I'm ready for that hug, Uncle Romo," Sarah said as she returned to the kitchen. "I hope you don't mind if I call you Uncle Romo. Will you be staying with us for a while?"

"I haven't made my mind up, yet. It will take a while for all this to sink in."

"Well, you're more than welcome to stay here as long as you like."

"Did you go by the funeral home?" Tyler asked.

"Yes. The director put the container on the floorboard of the car for me."

Sarah asked, "If you don't mind, honey, would you mind getting it out of the car? I just don't trust myself carrying that box, and it makes me feel weird to be handling it." As Tyler left to get the box out of the car, he said to Romo, "I have no idea where Dad would have liked to have his ashes spread. I never heard him say. He just always said he would like to be cremated when the time came. Would you have any idea, Uncle Romo?

"Can't say that I do, son, but I'm sure whatever decision you make will be the right one."

~ * ~

The following morning, Romo was up early and got his funeral outfit out of the closet. He had brought the only dressy outfit he liked to wear: gray pants, a navy blue sport coat, white shirt and striped necktie. He remembered the last time he wore that sport coat and tie was with Paul when he had gone down to Greensboro for the retirement party. Romo got dressed and walked into the living room where Tyler and Sarah were waiting.

"Uncle Romo, would you like to have breakfast? Sarah and I just didn't have an appetite."

"No thank you, neither do I."

"Would you mind standing with me and Sarah at the end of the service? I could use your support."

"You've got it, Tyler. I'll be right there beside you."

The ceremony lasted about two and a half hours and, after it was over, they stood and shook hands with people coming out of the church. Maria, Paul's ex-wife, walked up with her new husband, Eddie, and gave Tyler a hug. "I'm so sorry, son. If there is anything Eddie and I can do, just let me know." Eddie laid his hand on Tyler's shoulder extending his sympathy, and then said, "Come by sometime and see us, Tyler. Our door is always open to you and Sarah. I want you to know that."

Maria walked up to Romo. "It's been a long time, Romo. How have you been?"

"Until now, I've been doing good, Maria. And yourself?"

"Like you, other than this happening, we have been doing okay. I'm sorry, Romo. Paul is going to be missed by a lot of people, and I pray they find the one who did this to him." She took Eddie by the arm and introduced him. "This is my husband, Eddie Reynolds." Romo shook his hand with a firm grip that was reciprocated by Eddie. "I'm sorry for your loss,

Romo. If there's anything I can do for you, just let me know. I'll be glad to assist in any way I can."

On the way back home, Romo asked Tyler if he would go by Paul's house. "I would like to see where he lived," admitted Romo.

"We can certainly do that. It's basically on the way."

As they headed west out of Philadelphia, Tyler drove through a neighborhood that looked as though it had only recently been built. Tyler slowed and turned right between two brick columns. There was a row of two-story townhomes on the right with single car garages attached to them. Across the street was a family park with swings and sliding boards. There was a wide sidewalk winding its way through the trees and around a lake. People were walking, some jogging.

"This looks like a nice area, Tyler."

"Dad bought it new after he and Mom separated. He seemed to like it here. Sometimes, he would go walking over at the park, which has about a ten-acre lake in the center of it. Once in a while, I would come over and go walking with him, but it's been some time. Dad worked all kind of crazy hours. You never knew when he was working and when he wasn't."

Tyler pulled into the driveway. "I think the garage door opener is inside Dad's truck in the garage." Tyler used his key to unlock the front door. He told Romo, "I had to have a carpenter come over and repair the door after the investigation so I could at least lock it."

Romo, Tyler, and Sarah walked into the house and into the den. It was a very large room with a fireplace. Romo was impressed.

Tyler responded to Romo's attraction to his dad's home. "Sarah came over and helped him decorate it. I think she did a good job, Uncle Romo, don't you?"

"Sarah, you did great. This is a nice looking place."

As they walked into the kitchen, Tyler stopped. There was a small bar in the center of the kitchen with four barstools. Tyler pointed to a spot and said, "They found Dad between the refrigerator and bar. I'm sorry, Uncle Romo, we haven't had time to send anyone over to clean up."

Romo took his time walking around the crime scene. It appeared that nothing had really been changed or was out of order since the investigation. He had taken a close look at the repaired front door as they walked to the kitchen. "Tyler, do you think you could get me a copy of all the pictures and the reports from homicide so I can take a look at them?"

"Sure, I can do that. Are you not going home tomorrow, Uncle Romo?"

"I think I may hang around a few days just to see how the investigation is coming along. And if you don't mind, Tyler, I would like to stay here at your dad's house."

"It's a mess, Uncle Romo. Just come home and stay with me until we have someone come over and clean it up. Upstairs is a mess, too. No one has been here since the investigation."

"No, no. Let me clean it up. That will give me something to do while I'm here."

"Okay, then, if that's what you want to do. Dad's truck is in the garage. I'm sure the keys are in the ashtray. That's where he usually left them. If you'd like to use the truck while you're here, you're more than welcome."

"That would be great, Tyler. I certainly do appreciate it. Just don't forget to bring me that information as soon as you can."

"I'll make copies of everything in the morning and bring it to you sometime tomorrow afternoon. I'll also bring your suitcase, and everything you have at the house. Here's a house key for you. I don't know what's in the refrigerator. I'm sure there's a beer or two. He always had a cold beer on hand when I came over."

Romo stood there for moment looking around in the kitchen to see what was in place and what wasn't.

"I know you guys want to get back home, so y'all go ahead. I think I'm just going to hang out and watch television, and then go on to bed a little later."

As soon as Tyler and Sarah left, Romo walked back into the kitchen and observed everything from the entranceway. He was convinced no one had been back into the house after the crime scene had been investigated by the police. There were some bloodstains still on the floor, some broken glass on the floor in front of the refrigerator, and a small glass on the counter that was half full of water. He noticed some blood spots on the bottom of the refrigerator; there were shoe prints everywhere, probably made on the wet floor no one had bothered to clean up, which he believed would have been those of the investigators. Deciding to check out the bedrooms, he walked up the spiral steps and into the first one on the right. There wasn't much furniture in it; just a bed and a dresser. All the drawers had been pulled out of the dresser and thrown on the floor, although they were empty. The mattress was on the floor and turned upside down. He walked down the hall to the master bedroom where Paul had slept until just a few nights ago. There was a king size bed with four corner posts which had a stylish pineapple cone on top of each. It was obvious someone had been looking for something. Dresser drawers had been pulled out and emptied on the floor; the mattress was upside down and on the floor; the closet had been emptied; shoeboxes and shoes were strewn about the room, and clothes were tossed into a pile. Romo could tell that the object of this disaster wasn't just a search for money. It was definitely for another reason. He hoped to find out what.

Romo went to work putting everything back in order, inspecting everything carefully before returning items to their proper places. Two and a half hours later, after cleaning both bedrooms, he walked into the first bedroom and decided that was where he would sleep while he was there.

After a long sleepless night, Romo got up early and made a pot of coffee. As he was going through the cabinets looking for a cup, he noticed all the glasses and cups in the cabinet had been moved around. Nothing was in order. He knew his brother was a very neat, organized person and would have never placed those cups and glasses in such disarray. He stepped away from the front of the cabinets and onto a piece of glass. He reached down, picked it up, and looked at it closely. He then opened the first cabinet door beside the refrigerator and realized, the piece of glass in his hand matched the four remaining glasses in the cabinet. However, everything else in the cabinets was in sets of six. Romo thought for a minute. *So, one has been broken, and that left five. The other one is here on the counter, and that makes six.* He laid the small piece of glass on the counter and found a coffee cup. He was about to pour some when the doorbell rang. He thought it might be Tyler stopping by.

When he opened the door, there stood a short, stocky man dressed in a suit with a white shirt and a necktie. He was a muscular looking man in his mid-forties with an olive complexion and a short haircut. Down South it would probably be called a crew cut. Romo knew right away that he was from the Philadelphia Police Department. The stranger reached out his hand and introduced himself.

"I'm Lieutenant Frank Sparrow," he said. "I'm with the homicide division of the Philadelphia Police Department.

And you are Romo Lindy, Paul's brother from Greensboro? Officer Tyler Riggs told me this morning you're going to stay for a while."

"That's right, Lieutenant. Come on in and have a cup of coffee with me. I've got a fresh pot on and it should be ready about now." He stepped aside to let his visitor enter. "I haven't been up long, so please excuse the mess. I'm going to try to clean this place up today." Romo pointed toward the barstool and asked the lieutenant to have a seat.

Five

Lieutenant Sparrow observed Romo closely and said, "You're a big man, Mr. Lindy. Are all the police officers in the Greensboro Police Department your size?"

Romo knew by that statement that a background check had already been run on him. "You can call me Romo. Most of my friends call me Mo, but either one will be fine."

"Okay, Romo. You can call me Frank, but most people just call me Lieutenant. I just wanted to stop by and introduce myself, and to let you know we have everybody in the homicide division working on this case. Paul was a friend of mine, and I'm not going to let this go until I find the murderer."

"Do you think there was more than one person involved, Lieutenant?"

"Right now, I can't say, but to be honest with you, Romo, I think there was more to it than just robbery. After looking at the way the rooms were turned upside down, I would say they were looking for more than money. I want to tell you that we're going to do all we can to solve this crime, and we don't need any outside interference in this investigation. Do you get my drift?"

"I do, Lieutenant," Romo answered with raised eyebrows and a sideways grin. "I'm going to stay out of it as long as I'm confident that everything is being done that can be done."

Without hesitation, the lieutenant said, "I know you're a retired police officer, and, for the last five years, you were a homicide detective. It's in your blood, and I know what you're thinking. But I think you've got to stand down for now, excuse the military term, and let us do our job." Frank reached inside his sport coat and pulled out a folded sheet of paper. As he opened it, he glanced at Romo and said, "You have a pretty long record of being in law enforcement. Says here you were a Navy Seal for years, and, also, completed FBI training in Quantico. In addition, you were a self-defense training officer for the academy. After going to Greensboro, you married your childhood sweetheart and joined the Greensboro Police Department. Your success was followed by a tragedy. Your wife passed away from cancer four years ago, and just two years later, your mother and father were killed in a private airplane crash. They were headed to Asheville, North Carolina where they were planning to spend some leisure time at their mountain home."

Romo asked, "How much research did you do on me, Lieutenant?"

"Enough to know that with all your investments over the years and your inheritance from your parents, you are financially well-off. I would think a man with your means should be in the Caribbean somewhere enjoying life and not here in Philadelphia."

"I appreciate your concerns, Lieutenant, and I just might go to the Caribbean, someday, but for now I'm more interested in who took my brother's life. I'm not going to leave Philadelphia until I know the reason why he was murdered and who did it." The lieutenant could see by the look in Romo's eyes that he meant business; that he was not going back to Carolina until the case was solved.

Sparrow folded the paper and put it back inside his jacket pocket, took one more sip of coffee, and said, "Before I leave, I've got one more question for you."

"Okay. Let's hear it."

"On this printout it says you were raised in Greensboro. Paul was raised in Philadelphia and his last name was Riggs.

"I'm surprised that information was not on the printout. Paul and I were reared in an orphanage here in Philadelphia. We were sent there when I was about three or four, and Paul was about six. I was adopted by the Lindy family of Greensboro, and Paul was adopted by the Riggs family in Philly."

"I see. I'm sorry about that."

"That's okay. Everything turned out fine for us. Our parents had been killed in a house fire. Paul led me out of the house that night. Now you know why I need to see this through."

"I understand, and I get your point, Romo." Sparrow stood to leave and remarked, "You make a good cup of coffee. Maybe we can share another cup sometime under better circumstances. If there is anything you can do to help with the investigation, I'll let you know. I'm sorry for your loss, Romo. I'll keep you updated and will get back in touch as soon as I find out more."

Romo stood on the porch watching Lieutenant Sparrow walk to his car and thought how impressed he was with the man. He seemed very sincere, and he demanded respect. Romo liked those qualities.

As the lieutenant backed out of the drive, a little black SL 500 Mercedes pulled up in the driveway next door. The driver was a female wearing a pink baseball cap. She stopped, looked over at Romo, and gave him a quick wave. She then opened her garage door and pulled her car inside.

Romo decided it might be as good a time as any to introduce himself. He parted the hedges and crossed the driveway onto the sidewalk which lead to the front porch of her townhouse. He was about to ring the doorbell when he felt the suction of the front door get tighter as she opened her back door from the garage. He waited a moment, and then rang the doorbell. In just a moment, the door opened. There stood a stunning woman in her mid or late thirties wearing the pink baseball cap. She had on no makeup, was wearing jeans, a sweatshirt, and tennis shoes.

"Can I help you?" she asked.

Romo didn't know what to say. "Uh, uh, yes ma'am. I'm Romo Lindy, Paul's brother from Greensboro, North Carolina. I was here for Paul's funeral, and I've decided to stay a few days. I thought I would introduce myself just to let you know I'm staying next door in case you see some comings and goings on over there." Romo said all of that in one sentence without taking a breath. She could tell he was nervous by the way he stammered over the question.

"Well, you are definitely from the South. With that accent, there is no way you can hide it."

Romo ducked his head and said with a grin, "Yes, ma'am. Southern and proud."

She held out her hand. "I'm originally from Virginia, so, I guess you can call me a southerner, too. I'm Jessica Page. You can just call me Jessie. Everybody else does. Would you like to come in for a few minutes? I'm just before having a glass of wine so I can relax. I realize it's pretty early in the morning for wine, but I've been up all night working."

"You must work third shift."

"I guess you could say that. I work whatever hours are needed to get the job done. I'm an interior decorator, and I'm working on a building downtown, a seventeen-story office complex. So, the best time for me and my people to do that job is at night to avoid telephone and internet installations, and all the other stuff we have to contend with to get our job done."

"I can tell you're good at what you do by looking at the job you've done in your townhouse. Your place looks great. I suppose you do homes as well."

"I decorate some homes but not many. I do mostly office complexes, which house all types of businesses." She poured two glasses of wine and sat in front of Romo. "You said your name was Romo?"

It was too early for him to have a glass of wine, but he was not about to insult her by not drinking it. He replied, "That's right. Romo, but most people just call me Mo."

"Okay, Mo. That's what it's going to be for me, too. Did you have any questions for me?"

"I just wondered if you had heard anything from next door such as gunshots or any commotion going on last week about the time my brother was murdered."

"I'm sorry, Mo. I didn't hear a thing. I had gone down to Virginia to visit my folks and when I got back the yellow tape had been strung up all around the townhouse. One of the officers came over and explained what had happened. I told him the same thing I'm telling you, that I was out of town when everything took place. And to tell you the truth, Mo. I have lived here nearly a year, and I hardly knew your brother.

It seemed as though when I was coming up my driveway, he was backing out of his. He worked all kind of hours. Sometimes, that dirty police car he never washed was parked in his driveway when I came home. I believe there were times when he worked twenty-four hours a day. Sometimes, I would see police cars parked over there, and then other times I would see plainclothes people going in. You could tell they were cops just by the way they carried themselves, the way they walked."

Romo took a sip of wine. He watched as she stood and slipped the pink hat off and laid it on top of the refrigerator. She ran her fingers through her sandy blonde hair that parted in the middle and fell down to her shoulders. "That feels better," she said, as she sat back down on the barstool facing Romo. He thought to himself that she was not trying to impress anyone, especially with no makeup. By the expression on her face, he could see she was tired and needed rest. He also thought how easy she was to talk to and how she seemed to always have a pleasant smile.

"How long are you going to be staying, Mo?"

"Can't say right now, but I plan to stay as long as it takes for this case to be solved."

"I sure hope they find the killer. It makes me a little uneasy staying here now. If they would kill a cop, they sure wouldn't mind coming in here and killing me," she said.

"I really don't think you have much to worry about, Ms. Page. This was a personal thing, I'm sure of it, so don't worry too much about that. By the way, I need to pick up a few clothes. I wasn't planning on staying about two or three days, so I need to purchase a few more things to wear. Do you have any suggestions where I might go shopping?"

"The mall is the place you need to go and it's not far from here. As you go out the main exit, take a left, go to the first stop sign and take a right. The mall will be on the right. You can't miss it. There are several men's clothing stores there."

"Thank you, Ms. Page."

"Call me Jessie, please."

"Okay, Jessie," he said. "Thanks for the glass of wine. It's a little early for me, but maybe it will give me a jumpstart. I have a lot to do."

"I am sorry for your loss, Mo," Jessie commented. "If there's anything I can do, let me know.

Six

As Romo started back across the driveway to his brother's townhouse, he couldn't help but think how easy and casual it was talking to Jessica. He had not felt that comfortable talking to another woman since Mary's death. *She has a natural beauty about her. I think I'll go and find that mall. I need to pick up some more clothes, and it will give me a chance to find my way around a little bit. I'm sure Tyler won't be back until this afternoon, so I think I'll leave now.*

He opened the side door going into the garage and found a black Chevrolet Silverado that looked relatively new. As he slid under the steering wheel, he noticed the glovebox was not completely closed. When he reached over to open it, a lot of paperwork fell out. He slid over to pick it up and noticed a bright gold Cross pen lying on the floorboard. He wondered if the person going through the glovebox had dropped it out of his shirt pocket. He knew most policemen who had rank always used gold pens that matched their gold badges. Most policemen who didn't have rank wore the silver Cross pen that matched their silver badges. He eased the pen into an open envelope that was lying on the floor and placed it in the console box beside him. *Maybe I'm reading too much into this. It could have been Paul's pen.* He was going to hold on to it, anyway.

The keys were in the ashtray just as Tyler had said. He pushed the electronic opener over the sun visor and the garage door opened behind him. After backing out of the driveway and taking the left at the stop sign, he followed Jessie's directions to the mall.

As Romo pulled into the parking lot, he noticed that a dark late model vehicle had followed him. When he got out of the car, he glanced over in the direction where the car had stopped. He noticed there was only the driver inside. He shopped for about an hour and had chosen five pairs of slacks and five shirts. He had also passed a sporting goods clothing store, and decided to pick up a couple pair of shorts and some exercise clothes. When making that last purchase, he thought he might just take advantage of that jogging path around the park. He knew he needed the exercise.

As Romo was shopping, he noticed a young man wearing a suit standing in front of a store window with his back to him. He was across the walkway looking into a window where there were kitchen appliances on display. Romo smiled to himself and continued shopping. After Romo checked out, he walked across the wide walkway and tapped the young man on the shoulder. As the man turned around, he looked right into the chest of Romo. He slowly raised his head until he met Romo's eyes.

"When I leave here, I'm going across the street to do some shopping at the Food Mart I passed when I drove into the parking lot. I need to pick up a few beers and some groceries, and then I'm going back to my brother's house. Now, you can follow me over there or you can go back to where you were when you first started following me. Or, if you'd like, you can come to the townhouse, and I'll give you a beer." The young man looked at Romo with wide eyes and his mouth half open, not saying a word. As Romo started to walk off, he turned to the young man and said, "Tell the lieutenant I will be just hanging around waiting to see if he has any new evidence. You have a good day, young man."

After going to the grocery store and picking up a few bags of groceries, a six-pack of beer and a couple of bottles of wine, Romo drove back to the townhouse. Checking his rear view mirror, he was satisfied he was not being followed.

Romo had just put the groceries away and was about ready to open a beer when the doorbell rang. He opened the door to Tyler, who stepped right in. He appeared to be a little nervous. He was holding a big brown envelope by his side and a suitcase in his other hand.

"This is all I could find, Uncle Romo. I'll keep a check on the investigation and, as the information comes across, I'll make copies and bring them to you. It makes me a little nervous to do that, but if it helps you, I'll do it. I didn't look at them. I got a glance at some of the pictures when I was copying them and it almost caused my knees to buckle. So when you get through with them, destroy them, please."

"Thank you, Tyler. Whatever you do, be sure you keep this between the two of us. It's not to go out of this room."

"I understand," Tyler said. "Well, I'd better get going. Sarah expects me home every day around five-thirty."

"You had better go then. You know you don't have to explain to her what you're doing for me."

"Oh, no. This is between you and me, Uncle Romo."

"That's good, son. Thanks for bringing it by."

After Tyler left, Romo laid the envelope on the bar. He sat on the stool and stared at it for a few moments. He knew he had to look at the pictures as if they were related to just another homicide and not consider any personal relationships. He knew it was going to be hard, but he had to keep the main objective of finding the killer in mind. He couldn't think about that right then, though. He needed to take a walk in the park, clear his head, and get his thoughts together.

After he put on his new, name brand shorts and pulled the jersey over his head, he took the new Nike tennis shoes out of the box. Looking at them, he thought they sure looked bigger than a size fourteen. But after lacing up and tying the shoes, he felt comfortable. As he started walking down the sidewalk, Jessie pulled up in her driveway.

"Are you starting out or are you on your way back?"

"Just getting ready to go," Romo said. "Would you like to join me?"

"Sure. Give me fifteen minutes...time enough to change, and I'll be right with you."

Romo slowly walked down the sidewalk and stood on the other side of the road waiting for Jessie. She walked out just a few minutes later wearing white shorts, a white jersey and her pink baseball cap. As he watched her cross the road, he could tell by her figure that she had done that lots of times before. The sun was beginning to set and it cast a shadow over the trees that covered the walkways.

"Great day for walking," Jessie said.

"Yes it is," Romo agreed.

"I see you were able to find the mall. Did you get all your shopping done?"

"Yep. Got everything I needed and went by the grocery store and picked up a few things."

"Did you find everything you needed at the grocery store?" Jessie asked, making conversation.

"Found everything but Neese's sausage; had to settle for Jimmy Dean."

"What's Neese's sausage?"

"It's made by a local company in Greensboro. I think they only sell it in North Carolina. Yep, I got my grits and sausage, and now I'm ready to go," he added with a big grin.

Jessie started laughing. "I love grits. I've been eating them all my life. They don't serve them in restaurants in Philly, and none of my girlfriends and friends knows what they are." With a chuckle, she added, "All I can say is, they don't know what they're missing! You think you'll be here long, Mo?"

"I don't know right now. I would just like to see how they are handling the investigation on my brother's death. I don't have a wife and family back home waiting for me. I was married for eight years, but my wife passed away from cancer about four years ago."

"I'm sorry, Mo. Maybe I shouldn't have asked."

"No, that's okay. We had eight great years together. I had known her from childhood. It's just going to take time to heal. Then this thing happened to my brother. It seems as though I'm having a stretch of bad luck. I couldn't do anything about my wife's death, but just maybe I can do something about my brother's. How about you? I know you don't have a husband."

Jessie hesitated for a moment. "Had a boyfriend when I was fifteen. I thought I was in love but it was a teenage crush.

Nope, never been married. Never found the right one. I was always too busy trying to build a career. I didn't have any sisters or brothers; it was just Mom and Dad and me. They live in Richmond, Virginia. I've basically been on my own since I was eighteen. I came to college here in Philadelphia, graduated, and started my business here, and have been here ever since. I love the City of Brotherly Love. It has a lot of history, fine restaurants and good job opportunities and I have a lot of friends here. I guess you could say this is home for me."

"I'd like to go into the city while I'm here and be a tourist for a day. I don't remember anything about Philadelphia, although I was in an orphanage here with my brother."

"Oh, you were?"

"Yes. St. Andrews Orphanage. I would like to go back and visit the school one day. Can't remember much about it. When Mr. and Ms. Lindy adopted me, I was about four or five the day they picked me up. Paul was standing at the end of sidewalk wearing a big grin. He was so happy for me to have a mama and daddy, but I was sad to leave him. The only thing I can remember much about it is waving at my brother from the back seat of the car. We waved until we got out of sight of each other."

"That's heartbreaking, Mo."

"It all turned out great, though. Paul was adopted a couple years later by the Riggs family here in Philadelphia, and they loved him. At eighteen, I decided not to go to college. Earlier on, I had thought about going to Wake Forest, hopefully, to become an attorney. I joined the Navy, instead, and after five years of seeing the world, I was offered a government job in Virginia. After four years of that, I moved back to Greensboro, married my childhood sweetheart, joined the Greensboro Police Department, and worked there until retirement. My brother and I talked on the phone every other week. We had discussed spending more time with each other after I retired, but that's not going to happen now. It's something I've got to deal with."

"Well, Mo. It looks like we're coming to the end of our walk unless you want to make another round."

"Let's do that another day. I have some things at home that require my attention, but we do need to do this again sometime."

"I look forward to it. Just let me know. I love to walk around the park."

When Romo walked into the kitchen, the first thing he noticed was that brown envelope. He walked right past it and opened the refrigerator door, grabbing a beer. He opened it and sat down on the barstool. He had no idea what he was going to see or read concerning the investigation, but he knew there were going to be some graphic pictures. He took a sip of beer. He realized that in order to do the job he had to do, he had to put it in perspective. It was a homicide investigation, and no more. He took a deep breath and opened the envelope.

He removed about twenty pages: six sheets were pictures of the crime scene in color. The very first picture was of Paul lying in the floor on his left side with his head in a pool of blood. There was no expression on his face. It was just as if he had lain down and gone to sleep. All of a sudden, Romo felt a sickness in the bottom of his stomach that gradually went up to his throat. His eyes started watering. He tried to clear his throat as the tears started running down his face. His emotions took control. Anger overcame him. He promised himself, "I will get the son of a bitch who did this to you, Paul. I promise." Romo remembered the last words Paul had said to him at the airport before he left, and he felt that

Paul had an idea this was going to happen. He just didn't know when and by whom.

Romo quickly went to the next page. The photos were very vivid. Paul's wallet was lying on the floor beside his body. Everything in it had been taken out and scattered on the floor. The following two photos were of the bedroom. The next picture was of the front door; the other was taken from inside the room where the door facing had been split, confirming there had been a forcible entrance.

On the first page was the name of the homicide detective who had written the report. It read: *It appeared when the door was knocked in, Detective Riggs was on his way to open it, but had turned to go back to the kitchen to get his weapon. That's when the intruder shot him in the back of the head at close range. A twenty-five-caliber shell casing was found under one of the barstools. It appeared the bullet entered the lower part of the skull and lodged in his head. More details will be known when the autopsy report is received.*

There were no fingerprints found so we assume the intruder used some type of gloves. Nothing out of the ordinary was seen by his neighbors. They stated that they had not heard a gunshot or noticed anything unusual in the neighborhood.

Apparently, the intruder did not think anyone was at home. He shot the victim in the head, robbed him of his money, and then went through his home looking for other valuables. It has not been established at this time if other valuables were taken. The investigation is ongoing.

Sgt. Phillip B. May, Philadelphia Police Department, Homicide Division.

Seven

After Romo finished reading the homicide report, he picked up the pictures and walked over to the refrigerator. He removed the magnets and started placing the pictures in order beginning from where the door had been knocked in, to the photos of his brother lying on the floor with his head in a pool of blood, and then to the pictures of the bedrooms after they had been ransacked.

Romo took another sip of his beer. He sat at the barstool and studied the pictures. After a few minutes, he noticed in one of the photos that Paul's gun was in the holster on the counter. Also in the photograph, there was a glass on the counter that looked like it was half-full. Romo turned around on the barstool and looked at the front door. He walked to the door and opened it. Looking up and down the front door carefully, he saw there was no damage. It appeared as if it could have been kicked in by someone's foot. As he closed the door, he observed the repairs that had been made. He noticed that the only damage was to the doorknob lock, not the deadbolt lock.

Romo took a close look at the doorknob on the inside of the door. It looked like the plate around the doorknob was protruding outward, as if someone had pulled the inside doorknob until it broke the door facing. It appeared that it had been pushed open from the outside, but this was probably done to make it look like a break-in. Romo had known right away there was more to this case than just robbery. He drank the last swallow of his beer and opened a small door under the kitchen cabinet, looking for the trashcan to dispose of his empty beer can. In the trashcan, he saw pieces of glass where the beer can had landed. He took the receptacle from under the cabinet and set it on the counter. In it, he found a small amount of paper trash. He removed the trash, leaving only the glass in the bottom. After pouring it out on top of the counter, he realized that those were the fragments that matched the glass that was on the counter. He reached up to the top of the refrigerator and took down the small piece of glass he had stepped on and picked up off the floor the first day he was there. That was the sixth glass of the set, he thought.

He looked back at the two photos of Paul, and the position his brother was in. He was baffled. He had seen a whole lot of victims after they had been murdered, and suicides, too, but the position his brother was lying in was puzzling. Then he looked closer and, about six inches from the left side of his head, was a small pool of blood. It looked as though he had been on his back, but then turned over to his left side. To Romo, it was as if he were trying to say something with his body. He was on his left side with his head resting on his left arm. His right arm was lying at his right side. His left leg was sticking out and bent back in a position that had his foot resting under his right leg. It looked as if he had done this on purpose before he passed away...but why?

After reading the investigation report and looking at the photos, Romo realized there was a lot to think about. Why was an empty glass on the counter half-full of water; why was one broken glass on the floor, and then put in the trashcan; why was the plate behind the doorknob on the inside of the door protruding outward as if somebody had broken in the door by pulling it from the inside?

In reviewing the pictures, especially the ones of his brother and the angle at which he was lying, he admitted to himself that he had never seen anything like it. When people are murdered by a gunshot wound, most are lying on their backs or face down, and sometimes in a fetal position, but never in a position that Paul was in. It just seemed that he was trying to say something by putting himself in that position...but what? After a couple of hours, he wiped his face with his hands and ran his fingers through his hair. He was exhausted and needed to take a break. He looked at the clock. It was ten-twenty. It's early, he thought, but he decided to go to bed, anyway.

~ * ~

Three days had passed. Friday afternoon Romo decided to take the pictures off the refrigerator to give his mind a break. After taking them down, he placed them in the top cabinet over the refrigerator. He needed to get out of the house and decided to take a walk. After changing clothes and putting on his tennis shoes, he had just started toward the front door when the doorbell rang. He opened the door to a tall slender man with black hair mixed with shades of gray around the temples. He was casually dressed with a short-sleeved golf shirt. The caller stuck out his hand. "I'm Dan Robinson. I was Paul's partner. I worked with him for about three months in internal affairs before I had to take a leave of absence due to my wife's health."

"Oh, yes. I'm Romo Lindy, Paul's brother. Come on in."

"Looks like you're getting ready to take a walk or a run around the track."

"Yeah. That helps me think and get rid of some of this anxiety."

"I can understand that, Romo. I just wanted to come by and give you my condolences. Paul was a wonderful man, and I thoroughly enjoyed working with him. He was very smart and when he got onto something that didn't look right, he was like a bulldog with a bone. He would not let go of it."

"Yeah, that's the way he was. He never gave up. He would stay on a problem until it was solved."

"You can say that again. I hope they find whoever did this. The media is saying he was killed while he was being robbed."

"Yes. That's what they say. I don't know how much they found, but they tore the place all to hell looking for it. I know that."

"How many of them do you think it was, Romo?"

"I have no idea, but if it was only one, a lot of time was spent here, according to the mess made of this place. Can I offer you a Coke or something?"

"No. They told me at the station today that you were in town, and I wanted to come by before you left and tell you how sorry I was to hear about Paul and all that happened."

Romo didn't want to give Dan a timetable on when he was planning to leave, so he just thanked Dan for coming as they neared the front door. Dan said, "If there's anything I can do, give me a call. I'm in the phone book, and Tyler also has my number. Please feel free to call me anytime. I'll be around the house somewhere helping my wife, but to hear her tell it, I don't do a damn thing. You know how that goes." Romo just nodded as they walked out the door.

Romo walked past Dan, crossed the street and started jogging and thinking. He had completed the one mile circle before he knew it. He heard a voice in the distance; it was Jessie crossing the road.

"You want to go again?" she asked.

"I was just getting ready to walk it off."

"Would you like some company?"

"I would love some, thank you."

She smiled as she pulled her hat tighter around her head.

"You're looking mighty nice today, Jessie."

"Well, I didn't take time to take off my makeup, so if you look at me by the time we get around the course, you may not have the same opinion," she said with a laugh.

"I doubt that. I've seen you without makeup, you know."

"Yes, you have, and you're still willing to be seen with me," she said jokingly. "Haven't seen you in a couple of days."

"Yeah. I've been staying in trying to comprehend what took place, trying to make some sense out of it."

"Have you gotten anywhere with that?"

"It's caused me to have more questions than answers."

"Well, don't let it drive you crazy. Maybe it's time you took a break."

"Yes, I guess so," Romo replied wearily.

"Since you are not so busy, would you like to escort me to my open house Sunday evening downtown?" Jessie asked. "I finally completed the job yesterday and put the final touches on it today. Open house is Sunday at seven. There will be drinks, wine, champagne, and plenty of good food to eat."

"I don't know how I can handle good food. I sort of got used to beanie weenies right out of the can and fried bologna sandwiches."

Jessie started laughing. "I can definitely tell you need to get out, so are you willing to be my escort Sunday?"

"Yes. I would be glad to. You can count on it. Now, the big question is what do I wear? Is it formal?"

"You can wear a tie if you'd like, but it's not a formal gathering. Dress pants, sport coat, and an open shirt without a tie is fine."

"You're in luck, Jessie. I've got that."

"You're not going to have any problems. A lot of people will be there you can meet, and a lot of them will be single women."

"Well. It's been so long, I don't know how I would react around attractive looking women anymore."

"So you don't think I'm attractive?"

"Oh, no. I didn't mean it that way," Romo answered in a high pitched voice.

Jessie laughed out loud. "I know what you mean. You're going to do just fine. Although it starts at seven, we need to get there a little early. It will give me time to do my thing before people start arriving. So, walk over to my place, and we'll go in my car. Need to leave here no later than six. It's about a thirty minute drive."

"That sounds good to me. I'm looking forward to it. Thanks for asking me."

As they finished their walk and started back across the road, Romo noticed a car in his driveway. As he got closer, he realized it was Tyler's.

After saying goodbye to Jessie, he went inside and found that Tyler had made himself at home and was sitting at the bar.

"Hey, Uncle Romo."

"How are you, Tyler?"

"I'm doing okay, I guess."

Romo could tell by looking at Tyler's eyes that he had been crying.

Tyler continued, "Sorry, I guess I walked in expecting to see Dad and it made me realize I won't ever see him again."

Romo walked over and put his hand on Tyler's shoulder and said, "I know it hurts, Tyler. It's going to take some time to be able to live with it. You will never forget your dad, but just know it will take a while to get adjusted to it."

"How are you, Uncle Romo?"

"I'm doing okay, about like you." Romo made his way around the bar and opened the cabinet doors over the refrigerator. "I'm going to have a drink of bourbon," he said. "I think I need it to make me relax. I've been a little uptight the last few days."

"I understand, Uncle Romo."

"Would you like to have a drink with me? I'll make it light since you've got to drive home."

"Sure. I could use one of those right now myself."

Romo opened the top side cabinet door and set down two small glasses. He stopped and looked down at them. He realized they were the same pattern as the glasses that were on the counter in the picture, and that one had been broken. Romo looked around. Tyler was sitting on the bar stool only about three feet away from where Romo was standing.

Tyler noticed Romo's actions and, with concern, said to him, "Are you okay?"

Romo hesitated for a few minutes, trying to pull himself together. "I'm fine," he answered. Reaching into the freezer, he dropped ice cubes into the glasses. He took the bourbon from the top cabinet and poured the drinks. Romo turned to Tyler and asked, "Would you like to have water or Coke in it?"

"No. I think I'll just let the ice melt down a little bit."

"Same here."

"I came over to invite you to have dinner with me and Sarah on Saturday. I don't know what she's going to make for dinner. Don't tell her I said this. It won't be great but it will be okay," Tyler said with a laugh.

"I understand. But she's young, and she'll get better."

"Lord, I hope so," Tyler responded, which prompted a big laugh from them both.

They talked a while longer as they finished their drinks. Then Tyler stood, and said, "I had better go, Uncle Romo. Sarah will probably be home by now and will be expecting me."

"Thank you for coming by, and I'll see you Saturday around six. Is that okay?"

"You come anytime you want to, Uncle Romo. We'll be there."

Eight

After Tyler left, Romo walked back to the kitchen and stopped at the entranceway. He looked at the barstool where Tyler had sat and focused on the distance from there to the refrigerator. It was only about five feet. Imagining someone sitting on there with his arms outstretched, holding a pistol, Romo estimated it would be less than two feet from Paul's head. If the killer were sitting on that barstool, that meant he would be shooting upward, with the bullet entering the bottom of Paul's skull, and penetrating upward like the autopsy report said it had. Romo sat on the barstool and started visualizing what he thought could have happened. *If Paul was fixing two drinks, like I was, with his back turned to the barstool, that could be why one glass was on the counter with ice in it, and one glass broken on the floor. That would put him on the right side of the refrigerator where his body was discovered, and away from the refrigerator, and the broken glass from the other drink.* Romo took the pictures from the top of the cabinet and put them back on the refrigerator door. He studied the situation further.

As Romo analyzed the pictures and where the body was lying, he thought it possible to have happened that way, especially after looking at the position Paul was lying in. He looked at Paul's left hand to see if there was any blood on it from the broken glass. He looked closely at that half-closed hand, as if he had been holding a glass. His hand had remained in that position. Romo followed the side view of Paul's body downward, and noticed his right hand was partially closed as if he were trying to make a fist. His left leg was bent, and his foot folded back against his right leg about halfway up to his knees. As he continued to observe, he thought again that the position was odd, and that Paul was trying to say something with his gesture. Romo was certain Paul knew his brother would be there and would be doing exactly what he was doing at the moment. Paul had left him a message. He just had to figure it out, damn it!

After reviewing the pictures for over two hours and dealing with all the things that were going through his head, Romo realized he needed to take a break. It was time to go to bed to rest his mind as well as his body.

~ * ~

The next morning as Romo sat at the bar drinking coffee, he felt like he was onto something, but just couldn't put it all together in his head. He knew he needed to get it all off his mind for a while, so he decided to go to the mall and do a little more shopping, maybe pick up a few things to wear for Sunday afternoon. He had thought about wearing the only blazer he had brought with him to wear to the funeral. For some reason, that made him feel a little uncomfortable, so he decided to go shop for new clothes.

The mall was coming into view, and he looked back in his rearview mirror to see if he had been followed. As far as he could tell, he was not. Romo was about to get out of his car when he noticed an elderly woman walking among the vehicles to get into her car. As she opened the door, a young man, who looked to be about twenty, with a black hoodie over his head and wearing sunglasses, ran up behind her between the cars. He shoved the door against her as she was about to get in the car, grabbed the handbag off her shoulder as she was falling down, and started running directly toward the truck where Romo was sitting. As the robber started to run by the truck, Romo quickly opened the door, striking the young man in the face. The impact knocked him backwards, and he fell to the ground.

"Hold on there, young man. Let me help you up." The man was lying there with his sunglasses halfway around the side of his head, and his hoodie halfway on. Romo held out both of his hands to help him up. The hoodlum, not thinking, held up both his hands for assistance. Romo took his big fingers and placed them between the attacker's fingers, helping him stand. At that moment, Romo bent the thug's fingers backwards until he heard them pop. The man was back on his knees screaming with pain at the top of his voice. He got to his feet and turned to run, when Romo grabbed him by the back of his hoodie. He held the hoodie with his left hand and drew his right leg back, as if he were going to kick a football, then kicked the young man in the seat of his pants. Romo lifted him up off the ground and threw him down on the pavement. He jerked him up again by his hoodie, and then let go of him and pushed him away. The young man hobbled off, screaming in pain. Romo picked up the pocketbook, walked over and handed it to the elderly lady.

"Are you okay, ma'am?"

"I think so," she said, "except my knee is a little scratched up. Thank you so much for getting my handbag back. The way that man was screaming, I think it will be a while before he tries that again."

"I hope so. I think you may be right, though. You have a good day, ma'am."

"I will, and thank you so much."

After shopping for about an hour, Romo finally found a black blazer that fit and decided he would wear a white cotton turtleneck shirt with it. He thought that would look a little bit more formal than an open collar shirt and felt it would be just enough to wear to Jessie's open house celebration. He also picked up a light blue polo shirt to wear to Tyler's for dinner.

That afternoon about six o'clock, and after getting directions again, he pulled up in Tyler's driveway. When he knocked on the door, Tyler opened it, and said, "Come on in, Uncle Romo." Sarah met him at the kitchen door. Romo bent down a little and gave her a hug. "How are you, Uncle Romo?" she inquired.

"I'm doing okay. How are you and Tyler doing?"

"It's been hard, but we're getting by. Would you like to have a glass of wine or a beer?"

"I'll have a glass of wine, thank you." He had no more gotten the words out of his mouth when the doorbell rang. "That must be Maria and Eddie," Sarah announced as she went to open the door. Romo glanced at Tyler. Tyler shrugged as if to say he didn't know why his mom and her husband were coming.

Greetings were exchanged again. Maria and Eddie were very cordial. After having a glass of wine and conversing for a few moments, Sarah said, "Everybody is going to serve themselves, buffet style. The salad is over here, the spaghetti is over there in the pot, the sauce is on the stove and the garlic bread will be ready in just a minute. The salad bowls and plates are over here, so start whenever you'd like. We're family, so we don't have to be formal tonight," she said with a laugh.

After everyone was seated, Maria asked, "How are you doing, Romo?"

"I'm okay. I just hope they come up with some leads to find Paul's murderer. And once that's done, I think I'll be fine."

"Do you plan to stay with us for a while?"

"Just long enough until I feel they're doing all they can to find out who killed Paul, that is, if Tyler will let me stay around just a little longer."

"You stay as long as you like, Uncle Romo. I enjoy having you around."

Sarah looked at Romo and complimented him on the pretty blue shirt he was wearing. "Thanks. I picked it up at the mall today."

Tyler, grinning, spoke to Romo. "There was an accident over at the mall this morning close to where you were. You may have been there when it happened."

"What happened, Tyler?" Sara said.

"An elderly lady came into the police station this morning and said her handbag had been stolen as she was trying to get into her car in the parking lot at the mall. A man wearing a hoodie knocked her down, and she skinned her knee in the process. She said when she got up to look around, the robber was on his knees screaming and hollering. There was this big man standing over him trying to help him up, offering both of his hands for assistance. As the man who stole her handbag got up and started to run, the big man kicked him in the hind end so hard he fell back down again, right on his behind. The big man helped him up again and sent him on his way. The robber was all bent over with his arms crossed over his hands, hollering and limping as he crossed the parking lot. An officer was on hand and took the young man to the hospital. Medical personnel said all of his fingers were broken except his thumbs and his right hip joint had been knocked partially out of the socket. The lady didn't get the man's name who retrieved her handbag, but she said he was big and tall and had a mustache. She said he was a nice looking man." Tyler finished his story with a grin.

Everybody at the table turned and looked at Romo, but nobody said a word.

"How is he doing?" Romo asked.

"It's going to be a while before he snatches another handbag. The police officer said both of his hands were swollen so big they looked like somebody had blown them up like you would surgical gloves."

"I'm sorry to hear that, but it sounds like he got what was coming to him," Romo said.

Eddie remarked with a grin, "I think he probably did. I think that was exactly what he needed, and thanks to some good Samaritan who went out of his way to assist the elderly lady. That's always a good thing."

"I need a little bit more sauce on my spaghetti," Romo said as he excused himself and moved away from the table. He was about ready to sit back down when Tyler reached around his neck and pulled over his head what looked like a leather shoe string with a small lockbox type holder attached to the end of it. Handing it to Sarah, Tyler said, "Will you lay that on the counter for me, honey?"

Romo was inquisitive and asked him, "What are you wearing around your neck?"

Tyler explained he had to wear it all the time at the office. "The guys on the second and third shift have one just like it."

"Oh, it must be a jail lock key," Romo said.

Tyler looked at Romo and responded with a little hesitation. "No. The police department has leased a warehouse about five or six blocks from the waterfront to store confiscated goods that are being held until trial dates come up. Only three of us have a key...the two officers on second and third shift watch and me. When any kind of confiscated goods are obtained, they are taken to the warehouse, documented, catalogued by case, and then taken to the warehouse. If anything's confiscated on my shift, I have to go down, and unlock the door, and the gates, and follow that same procedure. Since there are only three keys, I have to have mine with me at all times."

"It must be a nuisance to have to have that hanging around your neck all the time," Romo said.

"It is. We try to keep the location of that warehouse as confidential as we can. A lot of stuff turned up missing in our other building. This is a new location, and we're trying to keep it as quiet as possible."

"I understand those things can happen."

Maria broke into the conversation. "Have you had a chance to see any of our city yet, Romo?"

"No. I haven't had an opportunity yet, but maybe I'll get downtown one day next week and take a sightseeing tour. I would really like to go by St. Andrews Home for children and see it again. It's been a long time."

"That would be nice," Maria said. She continued, "Paul used to stop by there, occasionally, and take toys for the kids on Christmas, and sometimes he would even play the part of Santa Claus. He would always have dinner with them on Thanksgiving. He was a thoughtful and caring man, especially when it came to St. Andrews. He would go over on Sunday afternoons and play softball with the kids. He always had a soft spot in his heart for that place. He loved it there, because it was the only home he knew as a child."

"I can't remember a whole lot about it, but I do remember that everywhere I was, Paul was by my side," Romo added.

"He loved you. He was so proud of you and all that you have accomplished."

After about another thirty minutes of conversation, Romo decided it was time he left. It was about nine, and he had to drive back toward town. He thanked Sarah for a fine dinner, said goodbyes to everyone and excused himself.

As Romo was driving home, he thought about what Paul had told him about the confiscated goods. Paul had said they wanted to find another location for them, but it was a little bit of a surprise that Tyler had a key to it. He was also thinking about the discussion with Maria and how she said Paul would visit the children's home on Christmas and Thanksgiving. He couldn't help but feel a little sad because that was the only home the two of them had known. Romo was glad to hear that Paul would go back to visit and spend time with the kids. He always had a big heart for small children, but Romo had no idea he was that active all those years later. The story Maria told simply confirmed what he already knew. Paul was a good man and a good brother.

Nine

Driving home, as Romo was about to make the last turn before entering the townhouse area, he looked in his rearview mirror. There was his buddy. Romo quickly pulled over to the right and stopped. He put his arm out the window for the vehicle to stop. When the car stopped, Romo got out and walked around in front of it. The driver rolled down his window. He was a heavyset man in his mid-thirties and had on black rimmed glasses. It was the same guy Romo had seen at the mall.

Romo stuck his hand out for a handshake. "If you're going to follow me day and night, I think we need to get acquainted. I'm Romo Lindy."

"I'm sorry, Romo. I'm just doing what I was told. I'm Gene Parrish. I usually work on the first shift, but tonight, I'm just trying to get in some overtime to make ends meet."

"I know how that is. You're welcome to come inside and have a cup of coffee if you'd like."

"Maybe some other time. I'm planning on checking out in a few minutes. I see you're headed home," he commented with a laugh.

"Were you the one who took the young man to the hospital today, Gene?"

"Yes, it just so happened I was pulling into the parking lot when he came wobbling across in front of me screaming at the top of his lungs. I took him to the medical center. He had a few broken fingers and his hip was partially knocked out of joint, but they say he's going to be okay. He's just not going to be able to run and grab purses anytime soon. But that's good. Maybe this incident will rehabilitate him."

"Did he file any charges against the person who did that to him?"

"No. He said he didn't get a good look at him, and I sure didn't see anything, so we have just dropped it."

"Come on by anytime, Gene. Most of the time I have a cup of coffee or a beer on hand."

"Can't tonight, but I might take you up on that sometime." Gene said thanks and pulled off.

The next morning, Romo put on his jogging sweats and got ready to go for a walk in the park. As he reached over to take the last sip of coffee left in the cup, the doorbell rang. When he opened it, there stood Lieutenant Frank Sparrow.

"Good morning, Lieutenant. You on your way to church this fine Sunday morning?"

"I wish I were, Romo. I've gotten where I can't rest and I can't sleep thinking about this case. Paul was a good friend and a good man, and I'm not going to be able to rest until this case is resolved."

"I understand where you're coming from, Lieutenant, but over the years I've found that you have to get some rest, and a lot of sleep, or your thinking process doesn't work very effectively."

"But there is a lot here that doesn't make sense, Romo, and I thought I would come by and ask you a few questions that you might be able to help me with."

"By all means, Lieutenant. Ask away."

"How long had it been since you talked to Paul?

"It was about five months ago when he came to my retirement ceremony at the Shriners' Club in Greensboro. He spent the night at my house and flew back home the next day. He was telling me then about the opportunity he had to go into Internal Affairs, and that he was considering it. He did say a major in the police department came to him personally, trying to persuade him to take the job. The major said they needed him in that area of responsibility, but Paul said he didn't like the idea of investigating police officers and snooping around in their business. Within two weeks after he got back, he called me, and said he had to take the job, but he couldn't talk about it over the phone. He said there was a lot going on in the department that had to be checked into, so he was going to see if he could help in any way."

"But he didn't mention any particular thing that he was working on?" the lieutenant asked.

"Oh, no. He wouldn't say anything like that over the phone, anyway, I know. That was the last time I spoke to Paul, until I got the call from Tyler that he had been murdered. Now, let me ask you a few questions, Lieutenant."

"Go ahead."

"Investigators said it appeared it was a break-in and a robbery."

"Well, that's what the report said, but personally, I'm not sure of that."

"Let me show you something, Lieutenant," Romo said as he walked toward the front door.

"As you can see, this is where the repairs were made on the door framing. The deadbolt lock was not locked. Supposedly, only the doorknob lock was engaged." Romo opened the door. "See the outside of this brass plate where the doorknob is?"

"Yes," Lieutenant Sparrow confirmed.

"See how it's been pulled inward toward the doorknob? Now, look on the inside around the doorknob. See where that brass plate has been pulled outward?"

"What are you saying, Romo?"

"I'm saying that someone jerked the door open from the inside until it busted the framework on the door. By pulling it open from the inside, the intruder avoided the possibility of being seen trying to break in. I think they were already in the house. I believe Paul may have let them in, and it was somebody he knew. And you know, Lieutenant, by the way they broke in the door, left his wallet empty and pulled open drawers and ransacking his house like they did, they were not only looking for money. They were looking for something else, and we've got to figure out what that something else was. What did Paul have that they needed? Did anybody ever find his daily ledger? You know Paul always wrote down everything he did each day.

know Paul always wrote down his daily activities."

"No. Nobody has found it."

"Well, maybe they found it and destroyed any information in that ledger that would have led to them being suspected."

"Romo, you've got my head spinning," the lieutenant said as he took his hand and wiped it across his face, the front of his forehead, and then the back of his head. "What I'm thinking is totally different than what you're thinking."

"Well, I've got something else I want you to think about, Lieutenant. You said Paul was shot in the lower part of his skull. Now, if you will, Lieutenant, move over to this barstool, the one on the end. When I got here, I noticed right away there was a short glass on the bar, half-full of water. I stepped on a piece of glass, and here it is." Romo reached on top of the refrigerator and took it down. "Somebody swept the fragments up and put them in the trashcan." Opening the cabinet door, he said, "As you can see, everything is in sets of six: water glasses, coffee cups, saucers, except there were only four of these," he said, holding up a short water glass. Romo didn't want to give away anything he had received from Tyler and the investigation reports. He had to present the information in a way that it would seem to be his theory and his opinion.

"Now imagine this scenario for a minute. Paul is standing in front of the refrigerator fixing himself and someone else a drink. He has a glass on the counter with ice already in it, and one in his hand, putting ice in that one as well, when he was shot in the back of the head. Now, Lieutenant, I'm going to stand here in front of the refrigerator. I am about a head taller than Paul, so if you will, point your finger to the top of my shoulders while you're sitting on that stool."

Romo turned and the lieutenant was only about eighteen inches away from his shoulder blades. Romo continued, "The glass was left on the counter. The ice had melted, and that's why it was half-full of water. I'm sure the broken one on the floor was the one Paul was holding when he was shot. Now, Lieutenant, when you check the autopsy report, I would bet money the bullet entered the bottom of his skull, because the killer was sitting on that stool, and he pointed the gun at Paul's head from the lower position. Now, I've shown you and told you why I feel very confident that Paul let a friend in, was making a drink for him, and when he turned his back, he was shot in the head. Whoever killed him knew Paul was on to something. They also knew Paul would not give up until he found the answer, so they had to take him out."

The lieutenant just looked at Romo. "I'm semi-off-duty and I realize it's Sunday morning, but do you think I could have a drink? A stiff one at that," he said.

"Got Jack Daniels."

"That'll be fine, with just a little water. Thank you." The lieutenant sat holding the glass of bourbon in his hand, lightly shaking it, and watching the bourbon roll around. He looked at Romo and said, with admiration in his voice, "You sure did paint one hell of a picture, and I think you're about ninety percent right. Just between you and me, I've got to start pursuing this case in a different direction and can't discuss this with anyone in the department. Hell, you don't know who you can trust anymore," he said as he turned up his glass of bourbon and drank it all at one time. The lieutenant took a deep breath and set his glass down on the bar.

"You've given me a lot to think about. Thanks and you have a good day, Romo," he said with a stressful sigh as he stepped down from the barstool.

"You do the same, Lieutenant. Come back anytime and keep me informed on how you're coming along with the case."

"I will," he said as he stopped, and looked down at the doorknob, and took a close look at the facing around it. He looked back at Romo, shook his head, and walked out slowly, closing the door.

As soon as the lieutenant left, Romo went out and sat on the front porch step and tied his tennis shoes. He got on the track and started running in a slow jog. He had a lot on his mind, questioning whether he should have told the lieutenant his suspicions. Was he right about the scenario of Paul's death? After jogging a couple of laps, his mind went to Jessie, wondering why he was so looking forward to seeing her and going with her to the grand opening. After his wife's death, he'd had no desire to spend time with another woman. Thinking about his wife made him feel a little guilty about looking forward to seeing Jessie and going to the open house. He finished his four laps around the track, and then went home and took a shower. He wanted to rest for a while and clear his mind before he had to be at Jessie's.

After getting dressed, he stood in front of a full-length mirror and checked himself out. He had on light gray dress pants, a black blazer, and a white turtleneck. He ran his hand through his slightly graying, black hair and took a second look. *Well, this is as good as it gets*, he thought as he turned and walked out to Jessie's house.

Jessie answered the door and said, "Oh, my! Look at you. I like that turtleneck. It's perfect. You certainly will not have trouble with the girls tonight, Romo. I can assure you of that."

"Well, I'm not going to see the girls. I am going to escort Miss Jessie," he said with a grin that showed off his deep dimples.

"That's right," she said as she invited him inside.

"Jessie, you look outstanding, classy, and I might add, very sexy." He couldn't help but notice the white miniskirt she wore along with a white lightweight jacket that fit tight around the waistline and moved lightly over her hips. She wore light gray high heels that matched the blouse with the collar pulled over the jacket collar. Her outfit was complete with a white pearl necklace and matching pearl earrings. "Man, you just look great."

"Why, thank you. Lord knows at my age I try the best I can to keep up with these young ladies' styles nowadays."

As they started into the inner city, Romo noticed a billboard that read, *Welcome to the City of Brotherly Love.* He couldn't help but grin to himself. After parking the truck in the parking deck, Romo got out, walked around the car and opened the door for Jessie. "I see you have that southern charm and politeness," Jessie commented while getting out of the car.

"Can't help it. This is just what I do."

When they walked in, the only people there were the caterers.

Jessie said, "Mo, take your time and look around. Make yourself comfortable. I've got to check with the caterers and make my final round, so I'll be gone for about thirty minutes. Be back shortly."

After Jessie had made her rounds on the floors and double checked everything, the elevator doors opened on the first floor. It was seven o'clock, and people were starting to gather. She browsed the floor looking for Romo. She spotted him standing at the bar with one hand in his pants pocket and holding a glass a wine in the other. He and two women were busy in conversation. She could see his smile from across the floor. *He is rather handsome*, she thought.

As she made her way over to Romo, one of the ladies turned, and said, "I understand this is your next-door neighbor, Jessie."

"Yes, he is, and he was gracious enough to escort me tonight." She added, "And I will be taking him home when we leave." All three laughed as Romo grinned and took a sip of wine.

"You ladies enjoy yourselves. I need to mingle and check on everyone."

"We'll hold everything down here, Jessie. You go ahead and do what you have to do."

Jessie looked from one woman to the other. She smiled, and said, "You ladies behave yourselves," and she walked away.

Jessie moved around, mixing with the crowd and talking to different people. Occasionally, she took a sip of wine. Romo noticed how professionally she acted and carried herself. When she talked, she smiled the whole time. He could understand why she was so successful. She had the right kind of personality, one that let you know she was truly delighted to see you and enjoyed talking to you.

Occasionally, Jessie would look around for Romo, and every time she found him, he would be talking to two or three people or in a group. Of course, there were a couple of women there, as well. *He certainly doesn't have a problem socializing,* she thought. He did stand out in a crowd. She couldn't decide if it was because he was so tall, or his handsome looks, or just the way he carried himself with such confidence. She did notice that he was a hit at the party, especially with the ladies.

At nine o'clock, the evening was coming to an end. Jessie thought it was time to find her escort. Looking across the floor, she saw Romo walking toward her with a woman she knew. As they got closer, Jessie noticed she had her left arm wrapped around Romo's right arm. Jessie called her by name. "Hey, Wanda. Glad you could make it."

"I wouldn't miss one of your gatherings for anything, Jessie. This is real nice, and you've done a great job as usual," Wanda replied.

"Thank you."

"But I must say, your date for the night has been a hit as well."

Jessie didn't even bother explaining the relationship between her and Romo. She just said, "Good night, Wanda, and thank you for coming."

"Be sure to let me know when the next one comes around, and I'll be there," Wanda said as she walked away into the diminishing crowd.

Turning to Romo, Jessie remarked, "Well, it seems as though you've had a good time tonight."

"I sure have. Everyone here has been so friendly. I wasn't expecting this hospitality from the north, being an old southern boy and all. One lady asked me if I was from Texas."

"You do have a nice southern accent, Mo. The people here are not accustomed to hearing it, but from what I saw, you had no problem expressing yourself with that southern drawl. Everyone seemed to enjoy it."

"This is the first time in a long time I've really enjoyed myself. Thanks for asking me to come along."

"It's about time to go. The caterers will clean up and lock the doors, so you and I might as well be on our way."

After a rather quiet drive home, Jessie pulled into her driveway, drove into the garage and closed the door behind them. "Would you like to come in for glass of wine before you go home?"

"A glass of wine right now would be good."

Romo never sat down. After Jesse poured him a glass of wine, he leaned up against the bar and took a small sip. She asked if he would like to have a seat, but he declined.

"I guess not, Jessie. I think I'm going to just finish this up and go on in. Thanks again for inviting me out tonight. It definitely was the best social event I've been to in a long time.

The last one I went to like that was at the Four Seasons in Greensboro for the Teacher of the Year celebration. It was the last event my wife and I went to together. We had a great time. Thanks for the wine. I guess I had better be moving on. I've got to call my nephew, Tyler, in the morning, and I need to have a clear head for that," he said with a smile.

"Thank you for being my escort tonight, Romo."

As he opened the front door, he turned around to face Jessie, and replied, "It was my pleasure."

She looked up at him with a soft look in her eyes. He knew she was ready for a good night kiss, but the time wasn't right, he thought. He reached down, put his face beside hers, kissed her on the cheek, thanked her again, walked out, and slowly closed the door.

Jessie stood there after he left thinking that was the first time she'd been turned down for a goodnight kiss from a man. She stood for few minutes, still a little stunned by what had just happened, although the kiss on the cheek was sweet.

Ten

The next morning Romo was up early. He rang Tyler on his cell phone.

"Good morning, Uncle Romo. I'm on my way to work. Why are you up so early?"

"Had a lot on my mind. There's something I want to discuss with you this morning before you get to work."

"What's that?"

"Listening to your mother Saturday night, I didn't realize how much Paul cared for the orphanage. Since he spent a lot of time over there, especially at Christmas and Thanksgiving, and supported the home with a lot with donations, I was just wondering if you thought that would be a good place to scatter his ashes." There was hesitation on the other end of the line for a few seconds.

"Uncle Romo, I never thought about that. Dad did care a great deal for the orphanage, and I think it's an excellent idea. I can't think of a better place."

Romo answered, "You think about it. We may need to call someone over there and see if they will let us do that. As you know, they have all kind of rules and regulations so they might not allow it."

Tyler responded, "I've met the administrator. I saw him a couple of times when I was with Dad. His name is Steinberg. I'll call him before going over there with Dad's ashes. I'll get back with you."

"That would be great, Tyler. You have a good day, and I'll talk to you later."

Shortly after lunch, Tyler called. "I talked to Father McConnell. He told me that what we want to do would be just fine. He suggested doing it around six or six-thirty in the evening while everyone inside is attending Mass. He said that would give us time to be alone outside with no interference."

"That's great, Tyler."

"Will this coming Wednesday afternoon be okay with you, Uncle Romo? I'll wear my suit and tie out of respect for Dad. I'll come by and pick you up. It's basically on the way, about a twenty minute drive from where you are."

"That's good for me. It will give us time to talk on the way over and back," Romo said.

"Looking forward to it, Uncle Romo. See you Wednesday about six."

As Romo was putting his coffee cup in the sink, the doorbell rang. *Wonder who that is*, he thought. He opened the door, and there stood Jessie. She said, "I'm going back down to the office complex just to be sure everything was cleaned up after we left last night, and, also, to make sure everybody's satisfied. That would give us an opportunity, if you would like, to tour the inner city. I can show you the Liberty Bell, Independence Hall, and Benjamin Franklin's gravesite. It's all right there together."

"That sounds like a great idea, Jessie. Let me go back and slip on my loafers."

"Today is a beautiful day," Jessie said excitedly. "It's Monday, and there won't be a lot of tourists downtown, so we will be able to get around pretty easily without a lot of traffic congestion."

"Sounds good to me. Let's do it." He got into Jessie's Mercedes coupe and moved the right seat back as far as it would go. When he got in, Jesse looked over at him. "My God, Romo. I'm going to have to look in the trunk to talk to you." They both laughed out loud.

After parking in the parking deck and riding the elevator down, they ended up in the lobby where the open house had been. After speaking to the woman at the front desk and some others, Jessie turned to Romo and said, "Let's go, big fella. We've got some walking to do." After walking for about a block, they ended up at Ben Franklin's burial site right behind the Holiday Inn.

They continued walking up the street and crossed into the square. There was the Liberty Bell, encased in glass. Romo was impressed. After reading and hearing so much about the Liberty Bell, he was looking at it for real. It gave him a sense of pride to be an American.

Then they walked toward Independence Hall. Romo turned and looked and, within the distance of a football field, there it was. He had always been a lover of history, and he was enjoying it. Without waiting for a tour guide, he opened the big white wooden doors of Independence Hall and started down the center aisle. There were nameplates on the desks of those who had sat in them during the Continental Congress sessions. There was a seat where George Washington had sat...Thomas Jefferson, Benjamin Franklin, all the great names he had read about in his school days and from studying history books. After reading all the biographies at Independence Hall, they quietly slid out the back exit before other sightseers had finished their tours. Outside in the commons area, there were benches where the public would gather and wait for the Senate to adjourn. Then a Senate member would come outside, stand at the doorway, and read out loud to the citizens, advising them what laws and bills had passed during the session. The info was then pinned up on a designated wooden board for all to read.

Romo and Jessie sat on a bench not making much conversation but thinking about the history they had just witnessed and admiring America's accomplishments. Romo looked at Jessie and commented with pride, "It makes you feel like a real patriot after walking through a place like this, doesn't it?"

"It sure does. It makes you think a lot about just how far we have come as a country."

Their concentration was broken when Jessie stopped talking. She was admiring a young couple walking up the gravel pathway in front of them, holding their daughter's hand. As they walked by, Romo looked at Jessie who was beginning to tear up. "Are you okay, Jess?"

He took her hand and wiped a tear away as it slowly trickled out of the corner of her eye. "I'm fine, Romo." She took a deep breath and stood. "Let's walk over to the corner and get a Philly cheesesteak. There's a vendor right across the street."

Romo agreed. "You definitely cannot come to Philadelphia without getting a street vendor's Philly cheese steak." They started walking, and Jessie was quiet. Romo knew something wasn't quite right with her. Her attitude had changed instantly when she saw the couple walking with the young child. He thought it best not to say anything, but he also was aware that Jessie had just had an emotional experience. He put his arm around her shoulders in a comfortable way, giving the impression he was there to give her comfort if she wanted to talk about what she was feeling.

As they were waiting for the traffic light to change, Jessie looked up at Romo and said, "Why did you and your wife never have children?"

He was taken aback by the question. The light had changed, and they began walking across the street. As they stepped up on the sidewalk, Romo took her by the hand, and dodging some pedestrians, pulled her to the side. Before he could say anything, Jessie said, "I'm sorry. I shouldn't have asked that question. Please forgive me. I don't know what came over me. That's none of my business. I'm sorry."

Romo was holding her hands, and he could feel them trembling. Sensing she was upset, he replied, "That's okay, Jessie. Calm down. It's all right. For now, let's get our sandwich, and on the way home, I'll answer that question with no problem." He smiled when he said it so she would feel comfortable.

"You don't have to, Romo. You don't know me well enough to answer it."

"I wouldn't answer that question for many people, Jessie, but for you, I will." He held her hand as they moved back onto the sidewalk and up to the vendor.

Jessie ordered. "One cheese steak all the way and a diet Coke."

"I'll have two cheese steaks all the way and two diet Cokes. Put one of the sandwiches and one of the Cokes in a bag to go, please."

Jessie said, "Are you going to take one home?"

"No, I'm just going to take one over to a friend."

They walked away, taking their time eating their sandwiches. People were passing them because of their slow pace. Romo slowly walked up to a car parked beside the sidewalk. Holding the bag of food in his hand, he tapped on the window. While it was rolling down, Romo set the bag in the right front seat and kept walking.

Jessie looked at Romo, confused. Gene opened his car door and stepped out. He hollered at Romo as he walked toward him up the sidewalk. "How did you know it was me? This is a different car." Romo, never turning around, just raised his left hand and gave a thumbs-up sign. Smiling to himself, he took a sip of Coke and kept on walking.

"Who was that, Romo?"

"A friend of mine I met on the police department. Lately, he seems to be wherever I am, if you get my drift."

"Do you think he's following you?"

"Oh, yes. He's just trying to keep me out of trouble."

"Well, that's something else you've got to explain to me," she said as they continued walking to the parking deck.

Not much was said on the way home. When they were in the garage at Jessie's, Romo turned his attention to her. " Okay let's talk. We'll start with my wife, Mary, first. We were married for eight years. The first five were spent just enjoying each other and life in general. We were very happy, but we realized something was lacking in our lives. That's when we both started thinking about having a child. We felt that was what was missing. As time went on, there was no pregnancy. She wanted to find out why, so we started going to doctors. After about a year, the doctors came back with devastating information. Mary was diagnosed with cervical cancer. As you can imagine, the plan to have children was forgotten, and all we could think about was treating her cancer. Thirty-six months later, she passed away. I think most of the problems she had were due to not being able to have a child. The grief and the cancer slowly took her life."

"I'm so sorry, Romo. I wish I hadn't asked."

"Well, I only choose to think about the good times we had and not the bad. It's best to focus on just the good memories," he said as he started to get out of the car. "Oh, by the way, the guy in the car on the street from the police department? His name is Gene Parrish. Lieutenant Sparrow, who is in charge of the investigation of my brother's murder, doesn't want me to get involved in the case. I'm sure he's the one who's having Gene follow me just to make sure I stay away from the investigation."

"Let's go in. I'll fix us a glass of wine."

Jessie poured the wine and set the bottle on the counter. She took a sip, and then pulled the barstool over to sit directly across from Romo.

"Sometimes I get a little emotional when I think about children. I'm thirty-eight. I don't have a lot of time left to be able to have them. I've put education and financial gain ahead of everything else in my life. Now that I've had success, and I'm financially secure, I realize that time has passed me by. I've always wanted to be a mother, but it seems as though the cards were stacked against me. I think I've waited too late in life, and it bothers me to think I may not ever have a child."

"I can see how you might feel that way, but you never know what's going to happen. You could one day get married and adopt a child. I could love a child that I adopted as much as one that was biologically mine. That may be something you want to look at later down the road."

Jessie looked at him as a smile went across her face. "It seems as though you know the right things to say at the right time, Mo, and that's why I care about you so much."

He bent down and kissed her on the cheek.

"Are you going to be okay?" Romo asked, taking the last sip of his wine and looking up at the clock.

Jessie smiled and nodded.

"Well, it looks like it's time for me to go. Thank you for the day. I thoroughly enjoyed the walk we had, the history lessons, and the glass of wine."

"You're more than welcome, Romo. I enjoyed it thoroughly myself. And by the way, thanks for being a good listener. Sometimes I need that."

"I understand. All of us do at times."

Eleven

Wednesday afternoon came, the day for dispersing Paul's remains. Romo decided to wear his navy blue sport coat and necktie, the same outfit he'd worn to the funeral. Once he got dressed, he noticed it was five forty-five. He decided to walk out on the front porch and wait for Tyler, who was due at six. He felt a little nervous about going back to the orphanage. He hadn't been there since he was adopted, and he wasn't sure how he would feel once he saw the place. The last memory he had of the home was waving goodbye to Paul as he and his new family drove away.

His thoughts were interrupted as Tyler pulled up in the driveway. Rolling down his window, he asked, "Are you ready, Uncle Romo?"

"I'm as ready as I will ever be," Romo said as he walked down the sidewalk and got into the car. He noticed Paul's ashes were there on the front seat between them.

Tyler glanced at his watch. "It will take us about twenty minutes to get there which should be about six-thirty. That will give us about an hour before it starts getting dark," Tyler said. "That should give us plenty of time to scatter Dad's ashes, don't you think?"

"I would think so."

Not much was said after that, until they pulled into the parking lot. Tyler broke the silence. "I think I'm going to go ahead and pull in near the ball field. It won't be that far to walk from that point to the entrance."

Romo got out of the car and viewed the baseball field. It looked very professional. He could tell a lot of hard work had gone into looking after it. The grass was dark green and cut very close. Evidently, they were getting ready for a game, because it had even been marked off. The bleachers behind home plate looked relatively new. He commented to Tyler. "It looks as though somebody has been donating money, because this is a very nice, well-maintained baseball field."

Tyler nodded and said, "Dad came over and watched them play ball all the time. He brought me with him a lot of times when I was small."

Looking back at the main structure, Romo said, "I don't remember it being this big."

Tyler explained, "They've added two wings to it in the last fifteen years." He reached in the car and picked up the box of ashes. "Let's walk to the outfield and scatter them around the edge of the fence. You agree with that, Uncle Romo?"

"Can't think of a better place."

Tyler opened the container and looked down at the ashes. With a deep breath, he said, "Love you, Dad, and I will miss you." His eyes started to water as he slowly began to scatter the ashes along the fence line. He went from right field to centerfield, distributing small amounts at a time until he ended up midway of left field. Romo put his arm around Tyler's shoulders. They both walked toward the pitcher's mound. Once there, they stopped and looked back. Romo hugged Tyler, and said, "I think Paul would be satisfied with our decision. This was home to him, and I think he's back where he would like to be."

"Yep, I'm sure of that, Uncle Romo."

As they got closer to the car, Romo saw a priest standing there. He was a tall, slender man with solid gray hair and red cheeks. Tyler recognized him as the administrator, Father McConnell. He reached out his hand and greeted him saying, "Good afternoon, Father." Tyler turned to Romo and introduced him. "This is my Uncle Romo, Dad's brother. As I explained over the phone, he's up from North Carolina to assist me with this."

With a sympathetic look, Father McConnell said, "It's nice to meet you, Romo. I'm sorry we have to be introduced under these circumstances."

"I appreciate your letting us do this, Father. I'm sure Paul would be pleased having this as his final resting place."

McConnell replied, "To be honest with you, Romo, Paul's are the first ashes to be dispersed here and, most likely, will be the last. He was very active here. He would come over and pitch balls to the little ones and sometimes play with them all day. He truly loved kids. He would also help in the cafeteria serving the kids, and he was a great Santa Claus to them at Christmas. He is certainly going to be missed. Everybody is at Mass now, so would you like to come in for a visit?"

"I would love to, Father. I was adopted from here when I was about five years old. I think Paul was adopted a couple years later."

"Oh, is that right?" Father McConnell seemed surprised.

"Yes, that was about thirty-seven years ago. It sure doesn't look like the same place it was back then."

"Oh, yes. Thirty-seven years ago, it was just this main building," McConnell said as he pointed to the center of the structure. "Yes, those two wings were added on, plus a third floor."

"Unfortunately, I don't remember much about it. I don't think I was here too long." As Romo spoke, he began to recall some memories. "The most I remember were the sleeping arrangements; my bed was beside Paul's. I remember him waking me up every morning and helping me get dressed."

"That was Paul, alright," Father McConnell said. "He was always helping somebody. He was just that kind of person."

"I would like to go up and see it one more time."

"You're more than welcome, Romo. Come on. I'll walk with you. Nobody is there now, so it will be a perfect time to visit."

Father McConnell opened the double wide steel doors and stepped inside. Before them was a wide staircase, approximately twelve feet wide, leading up to the second floor. "Oh, I remember these steps, but they looked a lot longer then than they do now," Romo exclaimed.

When they got to the top floor, Romo turned right. He opened one of the double doors, stopped, and viewed the bunk beds. They were lined up on each side of the wall, with the foot of the bed pointed to the center of the room, facing the bed on the opposite side. The arrangement left a walkway down the middle of the room.

"I see the floors have been redone. I remember walking down the center and hearing the wood squeak. Now, they look awfully pretty and shiny. The walls were painted a light gray back then. This blue color definitely looks better." As

Romo slowly walked down the aisle, about midway he stopped and pointed. "This is where my bed was..." he said, placing his left hand on the foot of the bed, "...and Paul's was here," he added, placing his right hand on that bed. "The beds aren't the same, now. Ours had tall posts on all four corners. That window between the beds let in enough light so I could see a little bit of Paul, and he could see me, especially if there was a bright moon. Paul taught me my ABCs by that light."

"How did he do that?" Tyler asked.

"He would hold his hands up in front of that window, and, at night, it threw a shadow on the other side of the wall. He would start off by saying this is an A, this is a B, and then he would place his hands to look like a capital A and a capital B. He would go all the way through the alphabet, and after a while, he would make the signs, and I would call them out. That was sort of our game every night until I went to sleep. Sometimes, if there were a hard rain or a storm outside, I would get scared. Paul would take his pillow and lie down beside my bed, and I would hold his hand until I went to sleep. The next morning he would be back in his bed."

Romo hesitated for a minute. He was beginning to get emotional, and it was difficult to talk. He managed to continue, and said, "Once in a while, I would be crying for some reason, and Paul couldn't get me to stop. He would ease out of bed, go down to the foot of his bed, and screw off the top of the bed post, which was about the size of a baseball. He would reach inside and pull something out. Then he would screw the ball back on the top of the bed post. He would sit on my bed and hand me a piece of gum. I think it was the kind that had two square pieces in a small box. He would give me one, and I would start chewing. Boy, it sure was good. Naturally, at that point, I'd stop crying."

"Where did he get that gum?"

"Lord only knows," Romo replied.

It was early evening, and the sun was beginning to set. Romo walked over to the window. He stuck his hand in front of the window, and it threw a shadow to the other side of the wall. He couldn't help but grin. Then, all of a sudden, he stopped, looked at Tyler with his eyes wide open, and an expression on his face that Tyler had never seen. Tyler knew something had gone wrong.

"What's wrong, Uncle Romo?"

"I just thought of something, Tyler. We've got to go. Thank you, Father McConnell, for showing us around." Romo led the way out. As they got to the car, Father McConnell shook their hands, and said, "You guys come back anytime. Would love to have you."

When they got back in the car and on the main highway, Tyler asked, "Are you okay, Uncle Romo?"

"I'm fine. I just thought of something I've got to check out when I get back."

As Tyler pulled up in the driveway, Romo jumped out almost before the car stopped. "You go on home, Tyler. We'll talk tomorrow."

Before Tyler could answer, Romo closed the door and went inside the house. He immediately went right to the cabinet and pulled out the pictures. He looked at them closely. He could not believe his eyes. There it was. *He was telling me who did it.*

Romo looked at each picture carefully. Paul's head was lying on his left arm. Romo followed it out to Paul's hand. His hand was shaped like he had been holding a glass when he was shot, but in reality, he was making a C-shaped figure. His right hand was lying by his side balled up like a fist. Romo had seen that figure before on the wall at the boys' school. It represented an O. His left knee protruded outward with his foot back against his right leg, which represented a P. Immediately, the thought came to his mind, and he said it out loud. "It was a damn cop that did this!" He said it again. "A damn cop did this." He was not totally surprised at his conclusion, though. Just by observing the crime scene, he had known it was somebody Paul knew fairly well. Paul had been in Internal Affairs where he investigated other police officers, and that meant it was a good possibility a cop had committed the murder. With certainty, he knew where to start his investigation: the Philadelphia Police Department.

After the discovery, Romo decided a jog around the track would relieve the tension that had just overtaken him. After changing clothes and putting on his running shoes, he looked at his watch. It was eight-fifteen. The lights went out in the park at nine-thirty, so an hour of jogging should do it. He walked out the door and crossed the street into the park. Without stretching first, he started off at a slow jog, letting thoughts flood his mind. He thought of the day's activities, spreading Paul's ashes, and then memories of being at St. Andrews crowded his mind. He thought about just how much Paul had watched over and cared for him. Paul was a wonderful brother. Romo wished he had gotten closer to him in the later years. It was too late for that, but not too late to make the killer pay for his brother's death. He swore he wouldn't leave until that was done. As Romo continued running laps, he felt the sweat running down his face, and his breathing grew heavier. The only sounds he could hear were those of his breathing, and his shoes striking the pavement. He was beginning his last turn before the lights would go out. He couldn't believe he'd been running for an hour and fifteen minutes. He slowed to a walk and, with the light of the moon over the lake, he had no problem seeing the walkway. As he approached the road, he looked up and saw the silhouette of a man standing at the top of his steps. Romo stopped and looked up at the person, trying to decide who it was. Before he could say anything, he heard, "Are you having a hard time finding your way back home, Romo?" It was Gene Parrish.

"Damn, Gene. You caught me off guard. Thought maybe you'd be gone in by now."

"I'm getting ready to. Just making sure you're okay. There aren't many people out jogging in the pitch dark."

"Yeah, I didn't realize what time it was. Would you like to come in for a beer or a drink?"

"No. I think I'll get on home."

"How long do you think you'll be having to keep an eye on me?"

"I guess until the lieutenant tells me to stop. I know it's uncomfortable for you, but I'll do the best I can to stay out of your way."

"That's okay, Gene. You're just doing your job."

After Gene left, Romo went back inside. He decided to take a shower and go on to bed. As he walked up the steps, he first stepped inside Paul's bedroom. He stood looking around and noticed that the headboard of Paul's bed was facing west, and the footboard facing east, just like his bed did at St. Andrews Home. He started to walk away, but stopped and turned around, looking at the bedpost, especially at the pineapple knob at the top. He remembered the way Paul would undo the knob on the bedpost and use that for his hiding place for his chewing gum. Once again, he started to walk away and stopped. He knew what he had to do. He walked over to the bedpost, reached up, and started unscrewing the pineapple-shaped knob. He laid it on the bed and reached into the hole on top of the bedpost with his fingers. He felt something. He pulled out a gold key with the

Number 22 engraved on it. Sitting on the bed, and looking at the key in his hand, he knew Paul had been thinking ahead, as if he knew this murder could happen. *The shapes and signs on his body were something he also did knowing I would be the only one to figure them out.* Obviously, he definitely was thinking ahead.

Looking closely at the key, he felt sure it belonged either to a post office box or a safety deposit box. When the bank and post office opened in the morning, he would find out. Placing the key in his wallet, he screwed the cone back onto the bedpost. He was sure Paul knew he was going to find this sooner or later. He was really anxious to find out what the key fit. He felt certain Paul was leaving those clues so he might help solve the murder.

~ * ~

Romo was up early. As he poured his first cup of coffee, he wondered if the key was for a safety deposit box. If so, which bank could it be? He didn't want to call Tyler and ask him. He was sure there would be too many questions he would have to answer. Knowing Paul, he would probably pick the closest bank to do his business. He would start there first. Romo looked at his watch. It was eight o'clock, and the banks wouldn't open until nine. He would go to Jessie's and ask her where the nearest bank was. Taking his coffee with him, he walked out on the front porch. Just then, Jessie's garage door started going up. He walked over to the edge of her driveway as she backed out. Looking through the rearview mirror, Jessie saw him standing beside her driveway. She backed up to where he was standing and stopped.

"Have you been waiting long, Romo?"

"Well, I didn't know whether you would be coming or going, so I decided to stand here and see which one came first." They both laughed.

"Just have one question for you."

"And what is that?"

"Where is the nearest bank?"

She hesitated for a moment. "There's a Bank of America right down the road. Go to the stop sign and hang a left. The bank will be on your left about a half mile away. I'll be back about three-thirty. Would you like to have an afternoon drink with me?"

"Can't see why not. That would be nice. Is there anything I can bring?"

"No. Come on over about four-thirty or five. I promise you will not have to wait in the driveway," she said with a smile, as she resumed backing out.

At nine o'clock, Romo pulled into the bank parking lot. He sat in the car until he saw a woman unlock the front door. "Okay," he said to himself. "Showtime." He went inside and walked up to the first window. A young woman with long black hair and a pleasant smile asked if she could help him.

"I hope so. Can you tell me if this is one of your safety deposit box keys?"

"Yes, sir. It is a Bank of America safety deposit key. If you want to open the box, I will have to have some identification first, and then I'll have to see if you are a second party on file that gives you permission to open that box."

Romo thought that might not be good. Paul might not have his name down for authorization. He handed her his driver's license. She walked over to a file cabinet, pulled out a file, and walked back to the teller window. "Mr. Lindy, will you meet me over there at that side door?" she asked, pointing. As Romo walked over, she opened a half door. "Come on in and have a seat, please."

Romo pulled out a chair and sat. The banker sat in front of him looking at the card she held. "It looks like it all fits,

Mr. Lindy. The only name on this card that is given permission to get into this box is Romo Lindy from Greensboro, North Carolina, 1945 Old Irving Park, 27455. She inspected his driver's license and then looked back at him. "It says here, relationship: brother."

"That's right, we are brothers," Romo confirmed.

"But his last name is Riggs."

"We were adopted by two different families; his adoptive parents' last name was Riggs, and I was adopted by the Lindy family."

"I see. It all looks good, so follow me, please." She walked to the main door and opened it. The safety deposit box was on the first row on the top. "You're welcome to stay as long as you like." She pointed to a desk and two chairs in the room, and said, "Feel free to use those if needed."

"Thank you," he called out as the helpful woman left the room. *Paul knew I would be here. He had everything set up for me to review. Now, I just need to see what's in the box.* Romo placed the key in the slot. It slid open. Inside was a wire-bound notebook. There was a folded piece of paper on the front cover of the notebook attached by a paperclip. Romo walked over to the table and sat down. He took the paper from under the paperclip and read the first sentence.

If you are reading this, Romo, it's because I expected this to happen. I just didn't know who it would be or when. I hated to get you involved in this, but I also knew you would be here, doing just what you are doing at this moment. The notebook contains my daily activities and notes. It's complicated, Romo. In one incidence that an officer took to court, a forty-five caliber gun that was in our new storage location was the shooter's weapon in a murder case. When they read the serial number, it did not match the one that was presented in court. The judge threw the case out, and the suspect walked free. He worked for Zanetti. After that, a special key was made for the gate and the door. Only three keys were duplicated: for first, second, and third shifts. Anything that was confiscated on each shift was inventoried and tagged by the officer who had the key. Only he could do that. It was his total responsibility, and no one else was allowed inside.

Now, this is where it gets complicated. Tyler has a key and is responsible for first shift. Yes, my son, Tyler. Of course, the other two officers have that responsibility on second and third shift, and all are designated to take lie detector tests every three to four weeks. All have passed, including Tyler.

There is a guy by the name of Tullio Van Zanetti, who is a captain in the mafia out of New York. He is of medium build and wears thousand dollar suits. He has a chauffeur who acts as a bodyguard. He will take anybody out that just looks like they might get in his way. Zanetti takes care of everything on the waterfront here in Philly. He's in charge of what's coming in, and what goes out. The union bosses do not make any moves until they confer with Zanetti. I feel confident he knows how to get in the new warehouse and out without being detected. That is what I was working on. So, I would say that's probably where you will need to start, with Tullio Van Zanetti. Do not hold back. Do not do anything differently than you would normally do in an investigation like this, and you know what I mean when I say that. Be careful, brother. Love you, Paul.

Romo didn't open the notebook. Instead, he folded up the paper he had just read and put it inside the notebook. He sat for a few minutes, gathering his thoughts, pulled his shirt tail out, placed the notebook in the back pocket of his pants, and tucked his shirt back in. In case anybody was watching him leave the bank, he did not want to have anything in his hands as he walked out. He laid the key on the teller's desk, and advised her, "You can close that box out. It is no longer needed. In case you didn't know, Paul Riggs is deceased." The teller looked up at Romo with surprise. "I'm sorry," she said. Romo turned and walked out of the bank.

On the way home, the name Tullio Van Zanetti continued on his mind. He had to find out more about this man. After some thought, Romo decided he might need a little help with the job. Only one person came to his mind: Hammy Lee. He and Hammy Lee worked very well together and the majority of the time, each one pretty well knew what the other was thinking. Hammy didn't look the part of a detective; he was about six feet tall and weighed about 250 pounds. His stomach lay over the top of his belt buckle and his pants looked like they were two inches too long, but he had good instincts. He knew how to read people by their actions. He could practically tell what a person was going to do before he did it. *We made a good team*, he thought, as he pulled up the driveway and pressed the button for the garage door to open.

Once inside, he fixed himself a bourbon and Coke. He laid the notepad on the bar and started reading Paul's notes from the first page. There were several pages documenting how he had sat and watched the warehouse, night after night, and witnessed no activity. Toward the end of the notebook, Paul noted that Zanetti's driver and bodyguard stopped at Starbucks every morning around seven-thirty. The bodyguard went in and picked up two coffees while Zanetti sat in the back seat of the Mercedes. The guard was in and right out in less than one minute. Paul had stopped Zanetti and his bodyguard on two occasions. One stop was made at seven-fifteen early one morning, and the second was the very next night at eleven forty-five. Zanetti became very irritated and threatened to go down to the D.A.'s office and file a harassment complaint.

Romo knew what Paul was trying to do by stopping Zanetti. He was hoping he would get irritated enough that he might make a mistake, and do something different, get out of his routine. Perhaps if he made a mistake, it would give Paul cause to arrest him. Paul knew he was treading on thin ice by harassing the guy.

After he finished reading, Romo walked over and pulled the trashcan out from under the cabinet, pulled the trash bag out, and laid the notebook in the bottom. He then replaced the trash-filled bag. As he rinsed his hands in the kitchen sink, he thought to himself that now was the time to plan some type of strategy, but first he needed to see what Mr. Vanzetti was up to.

~ * ~

That afternoon, Romo dressed in his casual khaki pants and black polo golf shirt. It was four forty-five and about time to have a glass of wine with Jessie. She opened the door as soon as he rang the doorbell.

"Hi, Mo."

"Hi to you too, Jessie."

As she turned to walk back into the kitchen, Romo could not help but notice how cute she looked. He commented, "If you wore that to work today, I know you had to turn some heads."

"Oh, no. I got home about four, made a few phone calls, and then changed into this."

"Well, you look mighty nice, Ms. Jessie."

Romo's comment put a big smile on her face. "I'm glad you think so, Mo," she answered as she reached into the cabinet and took out two wine glasses. As she poured the wine, Romo noticed the bottle was half empty.

She looked at him, and commented, "You look a little tired."

"I didn't sleep too well last night," he said. "Had a lot on my mind."

"Did you have a good day?" she asked. "You had no problem finding the bank, I hope."

"Yes, I had a good day, and your directions to the bank were perfect." Romo held up his glass of wine up for a toast and saw that Jessie was not wearing a bra under her yellow tight-fitting blouse. As Jessie touched her glass to his, he said, "Here's to health, happiness and prosperity."

Jessie smiled as they each took a sip. She walked over to the stereo and pushed a button. Marvin Gaye started singing.

"You've got good taste in music, Jessie. Marvin Gaye is one of my favorites."

"I'm glad. He's one of mine, too. We can go into the den. I have a few snacks if you'd care for any."

As he went into the den, Romo stopped and looked around. It looked as though he had stepped into a page from *Better Homes and Gardens* magazine. The focal point of the room was the fireplace. Hanging in the center of it was a huge black and white oil painting of Philadelphia at night. Candles burning on each side of the mantel cast a gentle glow on the painting. It set the tone for the rest of the room. Cherry furnishings projected elegance throughout. The camelback sofa, with its light blue paisley design, faced the fireplace, and set an atmosphere that would put a guest in the mood of total relaxation. The only other light in the room came from candles on the end tables as well as on the coffee table. The flicker of the candles gave the illusion of a slight shadowy movement in the room.

"Wow! What a stunning room, Jessie."

"I enjoy this room. It's where I come to read and gather my thoughts."

As he walked around to sit on the sofa, he noticed that the coffee table held two or three kinds of cheese and crackers, some with assorted garnishments. He felt she had gone through a lot of trouble and forethought to make the evening special.

Jessie was about to sit down when Marvin Gaye started his second song. "Can you slow dance, Mo?"

"Sure." He stood and walked around the coffee table to the center of the room toward Jessie. She reached up, put both arms around his neck and laid her head against his chest. Romo could tell the wine was getting to her, not only by the way it was affecting her, but because half of the wine had already been drunk when she poured him his first glass. Romo knew it was coming to a point where he had to put up or shut up, and he didn't know exactly how he was going to handle it.

After four years, he had not completely gotten over his wife, and he had not been in a situation like this. It was the first time he had held another woman. It felt good, but still a little strange. Romo knew the conversation he was going to have to have with her later in the evening, and the situation at hand was not going to help matters. He knew he couldn't back down now.

Twelve

Jessie raised her head from Romo's chest and looked up at him with passion in her eyes. Instinctively, he reached down and kissed her on the lips. He felt her relax in his arms as he held her a little tighter.

"Are you okay, Jessie?"

Without saying a word and with a slight smile, she just nodded. When the song came to an end, she didn't let go. She still had both arms locked around his neck. Romo looked into her eyes and put his right arm around her waist and, without much effort, lifted her and laid her on the sofa. Jessie was still holding him around the neck with both arms. All past thoughts in his mind disappeared. All he could think of were her beautiful blue eyes, her red lips, and her sandy hair billowing in waves down the side of her face and onto her shoulders.

He put his lips to hers, but this time, it wasn't just a light kiss. It was a passionate kiss that he had not ever had with anyone except his wife. He was feeling more loving than he had in a long time. Jessie pushed him back as she raised up and rolled over on top of him. She sat up, and never taking her eyes off Romo, started unbuttoning her blouse. When she got to the bottom button, she undid it, and let the garment fall over the back of her shoulders. Romo was amazed how perfect she was in every way. Her breasts were perfect. She had a small waist, and the shadows flickering on her body from the candlelight exposed every curve. Romo sat up to kiss her, and she began pulling up his shirt. Romo helped her as he pulled it over his head, exposing the hair on his muscular chest. She pushed him backwards with both hands until he was flat on his back. She lay on him with her breast against his chest and, putting her face against the side of his, she whispered in his ear, "I just want you to hold me for now."

He put both arms around her tiny waist and pulled her closer. He could feel the passion from her body. Romo lay there with one arm around her waist and the other rubbing her back slowly. Not wanting to break the mood, he didn't say a word. He gently rolled her over on her back and slid the small zipper down on the side of her skirt. Jessie raised up and he slid her skirt off. She whispered softly in his ear, "Will you spend the night with me?"

"I would love to."

~ * ~

When he awoke the next morning, Jessie was not in bed, but he could smell bacon frying. He eased out of bed and found his pants, but his shirt was nowhere in sight. Then he remembered it must be in the den. He got up and walked into the kitchen and found Jessie in front of the stove wearing his shirt. It literally went down to her knees.

"I like your skirt," he said.

She turned around and looked at him, and then down at his shirt. "Well, it does come to the knees. I guess you can call it a skirt," she said with a grin. "Would you like some coffee?"

"A cup would be great," he answered as he sat at the bar.

Jessie poured him a cup, and announced, "I've got bacon, scrambled eggs and grits. How does that sound?"

"That sounds great to me. I had no idea a lady living in Philadelphia would know how to fix grits."

"I'll have you know I've been cooking grits since I was a kid. When I lived at home, Mom and Dad ate grits about every morning, and I have them just about every morning now."

"Well, then. I guess you could say you're a country girl at heart."

"As you once said, I'm southern and proud."

Romo chuckled as a big smile lit his face.

Jessie put the food on the bar, then took a seat across from him. Before he began to eat, he said, "I hope you don't mind. I usually don't sit at the table with my shirt off."

"No. I don't mind at all. Since I am wearing your shirt, I'll forgive you this time. And, by the way, you look good without your shirt."

"Well, I'm glad you think so."

After eating breakfast, she poured them each another cup of coffee, and said, "I think we need to talk."

"Yes, we do."

Holding her napkin in her hand, she met Romo's eyes. She began slowly, choosing her words carefully. "I would just like you to know that last night was great. It was very fulfilling, a night I will not forget for a while. It's been a long time for me, and I chose you for lots of reasons I won't go into. You do have the looks and sex appeal I like in a man, but not only that, I feel confident you are a good person, one

I can trust. Now, after saying all that, I don't want you to feel obligated in any way. I would like to think it was a night that you needed me as much as I needed you, and we are both satisfied."

Romo took a deep breath before he spoke. "Those were some kind words, and I feel the same way. Last night was my first time since my wife passed away." Jessie's eyes went wide, and her mouth fell open. She started to speak, but Romo raised his hand, signaling her to let him finish.

"My wife has been dead for four years. I've never met another woman I thought I could hold and make love to. I was beginning to think I never would, but thanks to you, I was able to make a step forward. You have made me realize I can leave some of the past behind, and, maybe, have a life ahead of me. So, yes. It meant a lot to me. I do think it was something we both needed and with no obligations. And if you're okay with that, I am, too."

With a smile, she said, "You mean to tell me that I was the first in four years?"

"Yes. Don't let it go to your head."

"My, my, I must really have something."

"Like I said, don't let it go to your head."

"So, we understand each other, and we're okay?"

"Yes. I'm glad you feel the same as I do, and we can continue being close friends."

Jessie stood and put the dishes in the sink. "I think I'm going to take a shower now."

"I'm going to walk back over to Paul's place, take a shower and make a few phone calls."

As Jessie started to walk past, she stopped and said, "By the way, what I have here is your shirt." She reached down, starting at the bottom of the shirt and pulled it up over her head. She walked up close to Romo, reached up, and pulled the shirt over the top of his head. She leaned her body against his. Romo reached down and gave her a light kiss on the lips.

She looked back up at him with a smile, and said, "I've got to go to work," and she turned and walked down the hall.

Romo watched her, and said, "You look mighty nice, Ms. Jessie."

She looked back over her shoulder at him, winked, and gave him a smile.

Romo decided to go out her back door, cross over onto Paul's patio, and enter the back door, just to make sure nobody was observing him. As he walked in the back door, the phone was ringing. He hurried to answer it.

"Romo, this is Lieutenant Sparrow."

"Good morning, Lieutenant. How are you?"

"I'm fine. I just wanted to call and tell you I'd like to come by this morning if you're not busy. We need to talk but not over the phone. We'll take a ride when I come by."

"Give me an hour. I just need to take a shower and change clothes."

"Okay. See you around eleven-thirty.

"That sounds good to me, Lieutenant. See you then."

Romo was dressed and standing on the front porch when Sparrow pulled up. He was looking forward to what the lieutenant had to say. He got in the car, and Sparrow backed out of the driveway and drove out of the condo area. Not a word was said until he came to a stop sign. He turned left and then started talking.

"I'm going to take you downtown and fill you in on some things. I've found out what has been going on that I'm confident your brother was involved in. That's one thing about Paul. You could never figure him out. He would never tell you what he was working on. He kept everything to himself. After speaking to some of the guys in the Internal

Affairs Department, I found he had sat in on the lie detector tests that were given on second and third shift to the individuals who carry the keys to the warehouse where we keep all confiscated goods. But he didn't attend the test that was given to his son. Remember, they are the only three who have keys. Concerning the homicide case he'd been involved in, he also found out that when the weapon was presented as evidence of the murder in court, there was a big problem. When the serial number was checked, it was not the serial number of the gun the detective testified was involved in the shooting. The judge threw it all out of court, and the murderer walked out of the courtroom, free as a bird. I understand that really pissed Paul off, because he had tagged the gun himself and put it in the warehouse for evidence. He knew someone had made the switch, and I'm confident that's what he was working on. He was probably getting too close to finding out what went wrong, and that's why he was taken out."

Sparrow slowed as he approached the waterfront. Off to the left were freighters and cranes loading containers. There were guys unloading the freighters. Tow motors were everywhere loading tractors, semis, trailers, and trucks on the docks. It was a very busy morning on the waterfront. Three workers were shouting to each other to get this one, take that one down, move this one over there. They were totally disorganized, but things were moving. Cardboard and all types of trash were blowing across the road against the buildings on the other side, making the whole area look trashy.

Sparrow continued explaining, "All of this is organized by the union, but the union is run by organized crime in New York. The Gambino organization covers New York, New Jersey, and Philadelphia. The guy that's in charge of

Philadelphia is Tullio Van Zanetti. He's considered a captain. His boss is out of New York, and let me say, this guy is a first-class gangster. He will have you killed in a heartbeat with absolutely no remorse. We know of several people he has had killed, but we just can't get the evidence to convict him. He, personally, always has an alibi and can prove it."

After they left the waterfront, they turned right on Chestnut Street and came to a four-way intersection. The lieutenant pulled over on the side of the road and stopped. The streets were busy with pedestrians and heavy traffic. On all four corners of the intersection, there was a bar. Sparrow explained the bars were where all the guys who worked on the docks hung out and spent their money. The bar across the street on the left was a two-story brick building that looked like it had been built in the early twenties. All the windows on the lower level had been bricked up and all the windows on the second level looked like the shades had been pulled all the way down. The front door was in the center of the corner of the building. It had a small sign across the top of the door that read, The Four Jokers.

As they sat and watched the front of the business, people came and went fairly regularly, and it appeared that everybody knew each other. They were shaking hands and patting each other on the back as they went in and came out. Romo commented, "It seems like it's a very happy group, doesn't it, Lieutenant?"

"This bar is owned by Zanetti. He holds his meetings upstairs in that room with the last window on the left. No telling how many people have been killed up there; chopped up, bagged up, put on a freighter, and shipped out to sea."

The lieutenant slowly pulled out and turned right on Race Street approaching the upper-class section of town. He pointed at a Starbucks, and explained, "Every morning around seven o'clock, Zanetti and his driver and bodyguard, Jimmy Sisko, arrive. Sisko is as bad as they come. This is another dude you don't want to mess with. He and Zanetti pull up and stop in the street right in front of Starbucks. Sisko jumps out and goes in and gets two cups of coffee. It takes about fifteen seconds. They have it ready for him when he comes in. He throws a twenty on the counter and leaves. Then they head down to the Four Jokers."

The lieutenant continued his informative tour as he drove slowly through town. "We knew the guy that was turned loose on that murder case. Paul knew him, too. He worked for Zanetti. Afterwards, we found out the guns had been switched. The gun had just been stored in the new facility on Commerce Street four or five days before the trial date. We moved all evidence material into that building. The evidence room we had was not large enough to store the things we'd confiscated, particularly drugs, marijuana, and cocaine. We needed more space, and the new building fit the bill. We had to keep the location confidential, even within the department. Our drug agents were the only ones who knew where this facility was. Nobody knows how the gun was taken out. We had not even had the new keys made yet. That's when we changed all the locks and had a special type key made to open the gate and the door. That's when we came up with the idea of the issued keys being worn around the necks of the three officers who were supposed to have them. They were assigned to the administrative building, and they were held accountable for anything missing. If anybody needed to get in, they had to call one of those guys with the keys. They were sworn to secrecy of its location and taken down to unlock the gate and the door. All of this happened within about four weeks before your brother's death. The DEA had stopped a tractor trailer early one morning, and found it to be hauling two hundred two-pound packages wrapped in plastic and duct tape. That's about four hundred pounds of cocaine, and you had better believe somebody's ass is going to swing. Knowing Zanetti, somebody's going to pay for letting that get picked up by the DEA. Tyler opened the gate and the doors, so they could store the cocaine. So far, we haven't found any dead bodies. I'm sure, though, that the boys out of New York are probably stepping on somebody's neck right about now. I'm sure they're not just going to let this pass. So, why am I telling you all of this? If you had any plans of snooping around, it's not a good time to do it. I don't want you to get caught in a situation where you get involved in this and possibly get killed. So do me and yourself a favor. Don't get involved."

"Do you think Tyler had anything to do with this?" Romo asked.

"I would like to think he had absolutely nothing to do with it. But being a homicide detective yourself, you know you don't rule out anybody."

Late that afternoon, about six o'clock, Romo received a phone call from Tyler.

"Hey, Tyler. How are you?"

"I'm doing fine. Sarah and I are going over to the mall. They have a great little pizza parlor there. It's the mall right below Dad's townhouse. Would you like to meet us there for pizza? I have some information for you. We should be there in about twenty minutes."

"Sure, I'll meet you there. I know exactly where it is. See you shortly."

Thirteen

Romo walked into the pizza parlor and saw Tyler sitting in a booth facing the front door. He waved. Romo sat beside Sarah so he would be facing Tyler when they talked.

"I ordered two large pizzas with everything on them, Uncle Romo, and a large pitcher of beer."

"That sounds good to me."

"I went by the hospital this morning and got a copy of the autopsy report. I went ahead and made copies while I was there."

"That's good. I appreciate that."

Tyler reached down by his side, picked up a folder, and handed it under the table to Romo, who took it, and laid it between him and Sarah.

Tyler said, "While I was there, I ran into Dad's old partner, Dan Robinson. He said his wife was there for a series of shots and said she was just staying the same; she wasn't getting any better but wasn't getting any worse either. He thought the shots she was taking were helping. She has to get them once every two weeks. He asked how you were doing, and if the police had any new leads on Dad's case. I told him if they had, they hadn't told me anything. He said to tell you if there was anything he could do to just let him know."

About that time, the waitress set the pitcher of beer on the table. "The pizza will be out in a few minutes," she advised them.

Romo, looked directly at Tyler and asked, "What do you know about Tullio Van Zanetti?"

Tyler seemed a little shocked. "So you've heard about Zanetti."

"I know he's a captain in the Gambino family out of New York, and he controls the waterfront here in Philadelphia."

"That's right, and I'm sure he's involved in a whole lot of other things that go on here. Be sure you don't mention his name around town, Uncle Romo. He's the kind that will be on your front doorsteps wanting to know why you're asking about him. The guy is a psycho."

Sarah said, "Uncle Romo, please don't get involved in this case. Even the attorneys I work for are very careful what they say, and how they say it, when anything comes up concerning Zanetti. They are scared to death of him. They make sure anything they say on paper is not damaging toward Zanetti. Eddie told me that one time he was investigating a wreck at the intersection where Zanetti's bar is located. This guy pulled up to the intersection. Some man ran out of the bar right in front of him, and he hit him. The man died two days later in the hospital. The accident report said that it wasn't the driver's fault, so no charges were filed. That was about a year ago. The guy hasn't been seen since.

He left a wife and small child behind. Everyone thinks they know what happened to him, but nobody can prove it. So even if you have suspicions, Uncle Romo, just watch yourself and be sure you know what you're doing. Zanetti is somebody you don't want to mess with."

The waitress placed two large pizzas on the table. Romo remarked, "Now, these are nice looking pizzas. They look better than the ones we get back in Carolina."

"I think they have the best pizza in town," Sarah offered. "How do you like being in Philadelphia, Uncle Romo?"

"It's okay, but I like the slower pace back in Greensboro."

Tyler asked if his dad's place was working out for him. "It's just fine, Tyler. I appreciate you letting me stay there for a while. Hopefully, this case will be solved soon, and I can get on back to North Carolina."

"Are you planning on staying until it's solved?" Sarah asked.

"I can't stay much longer. I've got to get back. I have some business to attend to there, and I can't do it over the phone. But to answer your question, Sarah, no, another couple of weeks at the most."

"You're welcome to stay as long as you want to, Uncle Romo. You know that," Tyler said.

After they finished eating and said their goodbyes, Romo went back to the townhouse. Knowing what he wanted to do, Romo knew he was going to need help. And the only person that came to mind again was his old partner, Hammy Lee. He thought he might as well give him a call. Romo looked at his watch. It was nine-fifteen. He started to pick the phone up then he realized it probably had been bugged. *I can't go out because more than likely Gene will follow me anywhere I go, and I don't want to be seen.* He thought about walking over to Jessie's house but questioned doing so at that time of night. He hated to do it, but he thought it had to be done, and this was as good a time as any. He hoped he didn't get shot first.

With all lights off outside, Romo eased out the back door. He took a case knife with him to open the gate to Jesse's patio. He eased the knife through the small opening of the gate to release the lock and walked up to the French doors. Naturally, the blinds were pulled. He knocked lightly on the glass. He was getting ready to knock again when the patio light came on and one of the blinds raised up. Romo had to squat down so he could see Jessie's eyes. Seeing who it was, she closed the blind and opened the door.

"What in the hell is wrong with you, Romo?" she said excitedly as she stood there in her nightgown with a thirty-eight revolver in her right hand. "You could've gotten your ass shot off doing this."

"I know, Jesse, I know. Calm down, and let me explain."

"It had better be good. You scared me to death. I was getting ready to go to bed."

"I can't call you, because I think my phone is tapped. I can't drive to a phone booth because of Gene following me. I don't want to get you involved in any way with what is going to be coming down soon, probably within the next couple of weeks. I didn't want anybody to see me coming in your front door, and I need to use your phone. I can't use mine."

"What is going on?"

"I'm going to tell you this, and it's all I'm going to be able to tell you. The less you know, the better off you're going to be. I have some new information about my brother's death. There are some things I've got to do to get to the bottom of it, and it's going to raise one hell of an uproar in Philadelphia when I get started. And to be upfront and honest with you, Jessie, you and I cannot be seen together at all until this is over. If this thing goes down like I'm hoping it will, there may be some people looking for me, and you know they're going to be over here asking when you saw me last. There also could be some people here that are not the police asking you that question. So again, the less you know and the less you see of me in the next two weeks, the better off you and I are going to be."

"Are you sure you want to do this, Romo? You could get yourself killed. Philadelphia is not Greensboro. There are people here that will kill you at the bat of an eye and not think twice about it."

"I know, but this is something I've got to do. I need to use your phone in private if you don't mind," Romo said.

Jessie looked at him with her teeth over her bottom lip, nodded, and said, "I'm going back to my bedroom. When you're finished, you can come in and say good night."

As she turned and started walking down the hall, Romo couldn't help but smile. He watched and admired her small-framed body and was amused at her swinging that thirty-eight caliber pistol in her hand. He had no doubt she would use it, too, if it came down to it.

It was getting late, and he knew Hammy Lee probably went to bed early. He had taken over the family business, raising different breeds of hogs for the sausage industry. He had turned it into a very successful business. It was located down in Randolph County near Level Cross, North Carolina, not far from NASCAR legend, Richard Petty's house. The last time he had talked to Hammy, he had about thirty-five employees working full time, and about that many more part-time workers. He knew those kinds of people go to bed early, rise early, and are at work before daylight.

He knew he'd better get the call made.

"Hammy, this is Romo. How are you?"

"I'm doing good, Romo. How are you doing? I was sorry to hear about your brother. Have they arrested anybody?"

"Not yet, but that's why I'm calling."

"Is there anything I can do to help?"

"I can't go into much detail, but I sure could use your help for about a week up here in Philadelphia. I hate to ask you, Hammy, but this job is going to take some planning to get done. And it's going to be dangerous. I couldn't think of anybody better to back me up than you. If you can't spare the time to come up here, I understand. I know you have a lot to do there on the farm."

"Well, I'm not going to do a whole lot of work. I usually go in about seven and tell my foremen what I want done for the day, and they get it done. That's about all I do. So as far as taking some time off, I think I'm due for about a week's vacation, and as far as getting into a little situation like you're referring to, you know there's nothing I like any better. So yeah, to answer your question, when would you like me to come up?"

"Saturday would good. That will give me time to get you a plane ticket and a room."

Before Romo could get another word out, Hammy responded. "Plane ticket? Oooooooh, no! no! no! I don't fly on airplanes, Romo. My feet are staying on the ground. I'll drive and leave Saturday morning early. That should put me getting to Philadelphia around lunchtime Saturday."

"If that's what you want to do, that's fine with me. I'll have everything set up by the time you get here. I'm going to put you up at the Holiday Inn downtown. Get a pen, Hammy. I'm going to give you directions."

"Go ahead."

"When you come into center city Philadelphia, turn on Seventh Street. The Holiday Inn will be on the corner of

Fourth and Race Streets. I'll have you a room, and I'll be waiting when you get there."

After Lee repeated the directions, Romo answered, "That's right, but there's one other thing I need you to do."

"What's that?"

"Go by my house and pick up the suitcase Ms. Blackstock is going to pack for me. You'll need to go into the house and go to my bedroom. Pull the top drawer out on the end table on the right side of my bed. My buddy is in there."

"You mean that forty-four Magnum you carried when you and I worked together?"

"Yep, that's my buddy. Ms. Blackstock won't touch it, so you'll have to go in, get it and put it in my suitcase."

"So Ms. Blackstock is still with you?"

"Yep, she'll be there as long as she wants to be. I've made arrangements for that. Don't know what I would do without her. Now, Hammy, when you get to the hotel I'll meet you in the lobby."

"Mo, I'm really excited. I'm looking forward to coming up and seeing you again. It reminds me of old times."

"I really do appreciate this. When you get here, I'll explain everything and if you don't want to do it, I will certainly understand."

"Stop talking, Romo. I'm excited about this. I haven't had a blood rush like this in a long time, so I'll see you Saturday. Sometime around lunch, if all goes well."

"Drive carefully and stay out of trouble. You know what you're carrying and if you have anything on hand that you think we may need, bring it with you."

"I understand, Mo."

After they hung up, Romo eased his way down the hall. Jessie had her bedroom door closed. He knocked lightly.

"Come in."

Romo slowly opened the door and stuck his head in. The only light in the room was coming from the bathroom where the door had been left ajar, just to give a little light in the bedroom.

"Come on in and sit here on the edge of the bed," Jessie said as she slid out of the way to make room.

"Thanks again for the use of your phone, Jessie. I owe you for a long distance call."

"I don't know what you have planned, but from what you say, you could get into some serious trouble. Not only that, you could get yourself hurt, or maybe killed, and that worries me."

"Well, it could come down to one or the other, but this is something I've got to do for Paul. It looks as though the police have their hands tied. There's not a whole lot they can do without some evidence. I'm planning on providing them with that evidence so we can find out who the murderer is."

"So this may be the last time I'll get to see you or talk to you for a while."

"I'm afraid so. I don't know how bad it's going to get, and I know I don't want you to be involved in any way. Being seen with me at all is not good."

Jessie was quiet. As she looked up, she could see the concern in Romo's face. "Well, if that's going to be the case, I'm going to ask a favor of you."

"Just name it."

"I want you to spend the night with me tonight and just hold me. You can leave early in the morning before light, but for tonight I want you to be with me."

Romo laid his clothes across an ottoman in front of a chair. Jesse slid to the other side of the bed.

Lying on his side with his head on the pillow facing Jessie, he said, "I think this is the best favor I have ever done."

Jesse smiled as she put her hand on the side of his face. Romo leaned over and gave her a light passionate kiss on the lips. Then he put his arm around her and pulled her closer. Romo knew it was going to be hard to put her aside, but for a while, he had to have total concentration on the things that needed to be done. He couldn't afford to have any distractions. He had been in this business for a long time, and he knew he had to keep a clear head. There would be no room for mistakes.

Fourteen

Early the next morning, Romo looked over at the window. It was still dark outside. He looked at the digital clock on the end table. The numbers read: 4:30.

It was time to go. He looked at Jessie, still asleep. She was using his shoulder for a pillow and her arm was laid over his chest. He slid her arm down to her side and slowly eased her head down on the pillow.

After dressing, he walked into the kitchen without waking Jessie. He looked on the counter and saw there was a pad of sticky notes with a pen lying beside it. He pulled one sheet off.

He wrote three words. *Thanks for caring.*

As soon as Romo walked in his back door, he headed for the shower. He stood there letting the hot water beat onto his face. The name Zanetti kept coming to his mind. If Zanetti didn't do it, he was sure to know who did. Obviously, nothing went on in Philadelphia Zanetti didn't know about, so he was going to start with him. He had to put some kind of plan together. Romo dried off, put on his sweat pants and a pullover short-sleeved jersey. He went into the kitchen and made a pot of coffee. He removed the bag from the garbage can, and from beneath it, he pulled out Paul's notepad. Again he read Paul's letter that was attached to the front of the pad. He read it slowly and very carefully. He made every effort to concentrate on what Paul was thinking when he wrote it, trying to make some kind of connection.

It was 10:30. He decided to take a break and go for a walk around the park. Just as he started toward the front door, the doorbell rang. When he opened the door, there stood Gene Parrish.

"Well, how are you, Gene? It's good to see you standing instead of sitting in a vehicle. Come on in," Romo said as he stepped aside. "How about a cup of coffee? Just made it."

"That would be good. I have something I want to talk to you about. It may help you, or it could get you killed."

"Let's just hope it helps me," Romo replied with a laugh. He set a cup on the bar and started pouring the coffee. "I'm glad you stopped by. It's good to meet you personally and get to know you, rather than seeing you from a distance in your car all the time."

"That's what I came by to tell you. I've got to have eye surgery, so there may be someone else doing my job. I'll be gone for a week. It could be longer. Can't say for sure right now."

"Anything serious?"

Gene took a sip of coffee and said, "Just got to have a cataract removed from my right eye. Nothing major, thank goodness. I know you're having a hard time dealing with what happened to your brother. I didn't know Paul well, but everyone who knew him liked him. He was always cordial and nice to me when I did see him, so I'm going to tell you something that's being discussed in the department. Most of it is probably hearsay, but homicide is working on it. It seems as though they have everyone involved in it, so rest assured they're doing the best they can. But from everything I am hearing, and what I'm picking up from the homicide division, everything points back to Tullio Van Zanetti. You have heard of him, I'm sure."

"Yep, I know he controls the waterfront, everything coming in, and everything going out."

"That's right and that applies to most everything in the inner city. He also knows what's going on, and if there is a crooked cop in our department, he knows who he is." Gene set his cup down, and asked, "Have you got anything to do in the next hour?"

"I'm free all day. Have you got something on your mind?"

"Take a ride with me; we'll use my car. I'm off duty starting today through next week." As Gene stood, he added, "Now Romo, what we say and what we do has got to stay between the two of us. I have confidence you'll do that."

"I give you my word, Gene. It won't go any further."

"Okay, let's go then. The reason I'm doing this is to show you how well connected Zanetti is with the city. This guy has been here for a long time. He knows everybody in politics and everybody that has potential to be in politics. He supports and contributes money to their campaigns and, if they are elected, what does that tell you?"

"I know what you mean. Unfortunately, it goes on in a lot of big cities."

"I just want to show you what you're going up against if you decide to get involved."

Romo nodded, not wanting to say anything to Gene about him and the lieutenant being down on the waterfront the day before. As Gene drove into the inner city, he remarked, "It may take us longer than an hour because it seems as though there are more cars out today than usual."

"Where are you from originally, Gene?"

Gene's glasses had slid down on his nose and before he answered, he pushed the glasses back up where he could see and looked over at Romo. "I'm originally from Worcester, Massachusetts."

"I can you tell you're not from here. I would have guessed you were from Massachusetts just by the way you said *car*."

"Yes, I still have that accent although I've been here about twelve years. With that slow southern drawl you have, Romo, there's no doubt you are from the south."

In a moment, Gene made a left turn. "This is Commerce Street, and this building coming up on my left is the new warehouse where all the confiscated goods are located."

Romo was a little surprised. It was a solid brick building with no windows. It looked like a substation for the telephone company. One level was about twelve feet tall with a steel double door in the front. Beside the steel double door was a single door entrance which also looked like steel. It had a twelve foot high steel fence with curled barb wire circling the top and went around the perimeter of the facility. There was a little patch of woods across the street in front of it with a house here and there. You would not suspect what it was being used for; it just appeared to be an old abandoned building.

"You definitely would not think that building was holding the contents it has inside," Romo said.

"That was the idea," Gene explained as he continued driving. "Now, when I get to this last light down here, I'm going to take a right. Everything to my left for about three-fourths of a mile is where all the loading and unloading takes place. And Zanetti is in charge of all of it."

Romo observed that all the buildings on his right were two and three stories tall. They looked as though they had been built back in the late seventeenth or early eighteenth century. Cobblestone sidewalks followed the old buildings all the way down the street. Trash from the ships and cargo boats had blown across the street up to the front of the buildings. Driving slowly down the street, Gene pointed to one of the old two-story buildings. He advised Romo that, back in the seventeen hundreds, those buildings were used for storing cotton bales that came up from the south to be shipped to England.

Gene continued explaining. "Zanetti owns that building and two more just like it. He bought them for nearly nothing. He heard the city was going to tear them down because they were not safe, so he went uptown, and talked the city government into selling them to him for one dollar apiece, on the condition that he would repair them. He told them he would. What does he do? He puts those stainless steel sliding doors in front of them. Inside, he poured concrete floors and then poured concrete right over the cobblestone sidewalks leading into them. The town went nuts, especially the historical society. They were trying to make him remove the concrete from the cobblestone sidewalks. He basically just told the city and the historical society to kiss his ass. He said he was not going to do any of that, and he didn't, as you can see."

Gene pulled up to the next light and stopped. He looked across the street and standing on the corner was Zanetti himself. "Look! Look, there stands Zanetti. He's the one with the dark suit on." His suit coat was unbuttoned and his hands were on his hips. He had a cigar in his mouth. He looked to be about six feet tall and in his mid-fifties. His hair was gray on each side up to his temples. He looked very distinguished.

Standing beside Zanetti were two other men; one had a white shirt on with his sleeves rolled up to his elbow. His suit coat was folded across his right arm. The other man was standing with his arms folded. He had on a gray uniform with some type of signature over the pocket. He was watching all the movement across the street.

Gene commented, "The big guy standing beside him with his arms folded is the union supervisor. And he does whatever Zanetti wants him to do."

The light changed and Gene pulled off slowly. Romo wanted to get a good look at Zanetti. As they went by, Romo was sizing Zanetti up and Zanetti was staring at Romo. Neither one turned away until they got to the next light.

"Damn. Romo, did you get a good look at him?"

"Yes, I did, and I think he got a good look at me too."

"I would say so, by the way you two were looking at each other."

"He's a very distinguished looking gentlemen. He looked like a professional businessman to me."

"He is a professional...a professional killer." Gene turned right at the next light. "On the right is his third building. I don't know that he uses that one, although it does have the new steel doors on it."

"What does he use those other buildings for?"

"When the ships come in and the owners of the cargo are not there to pick it up, Zanetti has the dock loaders take it right across the street with a forklift and put it in his warehouses. Now this is where he takes advantage of the owner. When the owner comes to pick up the cargo, they tell him it's in one of their warehouses, so the guy comes with his tractor trailer. Zanetti's guys load the truck for him, and the guy gets charged for double loading, rent on the warehouse space, and all the other things they can tack on to his invoice. So in other words, Zanetti is paid double. That goes on all the time. He's making a killing, he and the union. Now, the businesses that are paying that money don't say a word. They know if they do, it's going to cost them more the next time. They just add it as a loss and file it on their taxes. At the end of the year, everybody's happy and the taxpayer takes the fall."

Gene began driving out of the city into the suburbs. Romo had no idea what was on Gene's mind, so he asked, "Where are we going now?"

"There are another couple places I'm going to show you. It won't take long."

"How do you know so much about Zanetti, Gene?"

"The first of the year, January 1, as a matter-of-fact, the police department started a new task force to investigate organized crime. There were eight of us, and no one was supposed to know what we were doing. My assignment was to follow Zanetti just to see what his daily activities were, such as where he was going, and who he was seeing. Then we would meet at the fourth precinct at the end of the week and compare notes. After sharing information with everybody, we would see what we could tie together with our assignments for that week. After about four weeks, some patterns started to develop. We found that Zanetti was talking to the captains of the cargo ships and freighters and was getting them to stall out at sea. Then he would call the owners of the cargo and tell them it was going to be a day late. Naturally, it would come in that night and Zanetti would load up his warehouses with their goods. Then when the owners came to pick up the load the next day, he would charge double, and sometimes three times more than he should. But he would spread it out so as not to draw attention. By doing it that way, nobody would call the port authorities. The money was going to the union and in his back pocket, and a portion of it was going to New York. The way it was handled, it was hard to pin Zanetti down. If you talked to the captains of the ships, they would just say the sea was rough, and they had to slow down, which made them late getting into port.

"After about three months, we thought we had gathered enough evidence. In another couple of months, we were sure we could have nailed Zanetti and his associates. But, all of a sudden, we were called to a meeting and told our captain had been transferred. The unit was then dissolved, and we were assigned to two separate divisions. That was the end of our task force. So, to answer your question, I spent a lot of days and nights just following him around." Looking over at Romo and pushing his glasses back up on his nose, Gene added, "And he never detected that I was following him."

Gene drove out into the rural area and then headed west toward the town of King of Prussia. As they were riding along, Gene took a right turn between two huge rock columns. In gold letters on the side of a column, the words P.C.C, Philadelphia Country Club, a PGA Course, were imprinted.

Romo commented, "So, I guess he plays golf."

"Oh, yes he does and with all the politicians and the people with money in Philadelphia. He has one hell of a setup. You know that old saying that it's not what you know, it's who you know."

Romo looked out the window at all the fine homes, most of which would be valued well over one million dollars. "He certainly lives in a nice neighborhood," Romo said as they approached a slight hill.

As they rounded a curve, Gene pointed out the house coming up on the left as Zanetti's. "Now, that is one hell of a house," Romo exclaimed.

Gene replied, "All these houses sit on about five acre lots. I heard that the square footage in his house is about ten thousand feet." It was a light beige, three-story, Spanish architecture, stucco house with orange Spanish roof tile.

Romo was in awe. He commented, "It looks to me like all of them are about ten thousand square feet."

"There are some houses bigger than that, but I don't know who owns them," Gene added.

As Gene made a left turn and went around a sharp curve, he said, "See that house right there?" He pointed to the left side of the street. Romo bent down to look out the window to get a good look. Gene said, "That one is Zanetti's longtime girlfriend's house. She's only about thirty-five and, from what I understand, she's gorgeous. Now get this. The lot that this house is on backs up to Zanetti's five acre lot and home. So, if his wife is gone or out of town, he can just walk out his back door and right into the back door of his girlfriend's house."

"Well, that makes it convenient. The guy sure puts a lot of forethought in everything he does," Romo said.

"She's been there for about a year, and his wife knows absolutely nothing about it. Of course, this is not unusual. Most of those guys in the Mafia have girlfriends, but they all treat their wives with respect and give them whatever they want. That's one thing about their wives. They don't ask questions. I'm sure they know, but they will never ask. The husbands are seen in restaurants having dinner with the girlfriends and at other places. They are certainly not afraid to show them off."

Gene looked down at his watch. "Well, it's nearly one. I had better get you back. I know I've shown you more than maybe I should but, if Paul was my brother, and if somebody did to him like they did to yours, yes, I would do my best to find out who. If what I've told you and showed today helps in any way, I'm just glad I could do it."

"Gene, you have been a big help. I know now why it's so difficult to gather evidence to indict Zanetti. It's not going to be easy, and it's going to take time. I've just got to think about this."

There was not much conversation until they got back to Paul's townhouse. As they pulled into the driveway, Romo shook Gene's hand and asked, "Would you like to come in for a beer or a drink?"

"I appreciate it, Romo, but I've got to go downtown and see my wife for a few minutes. She works for the city as a notary. She notarizes all the land acquisitions and does the filing."

"Oh, now I know how you found out about the purchases Zanetti makes downtown."

Gene looked at Romo with a smile and a wink and remarked, "Like I said, this is between you and me."

"You have my word on it, and I do appreciate it," Romo answered as he opened the car door and stepped out. He quickly went inside, pulled out the trashcan and took out the pad of Paul's notes. He turned to a clean page and started making notes. He wrote down the number of warehouses, and where they were located on the waterfront, the directions going out to Zanetti's home and house number, Zanetti's girlfriend's house number he had memorized, and all the information Gene had given him. He was careful not to put Gene's name on the notepad. Next, he needed to call Tyler because there were a few questions he needed to ask. He was hoping they could meet after Tyler got off work.

Fifteen

"Hey, Tyler, I was just wondering if you would meet me at the mall at that pizza parlor."

"Hold on just a minute."

After several seconds of silence, Tyler came back. "Sure, Uncle Romo. I can be there in about twenty minutes."

"I hope I'm not interrupting your evening."

"No. Sarah said it would give her time to do some paperwork she had to have ready in the morning for the office."

"Okay, I'll see you in about twenty minutes."

Romo picked up the notepad and started out the door. He stopped, thinking that if he started taking notes, Tyler might think it was a formal investigation. Romo wanted it to appear to be a casual conversation, so he took the notepad back to the trashcan.

When Romo walked into the pizza parlor, Tyler was already there sitting in a booth. "Hey, Tyler. Thanks for coming."

"Thanks for inviting me out. I'm glad you called. Sarah seem to be in a bad mood, and you gave me a great excuse to get out."

"She must have had a bad day at work."

"I don't know what it is. Some days it just doesn't pay to say a word." About that time the waiter walked over and asked if they were ready to order. "I'll have a large Budweiser," Romo responded.

"I'll have the same thing. I went ahead and ordered us a large pizza with everything on it. Hope you don't mind."

"No. That's fine with me."

"So, what have you got on your mind, Uncle Romo?"

"From what I have heard and from reading the paper, it seems as though Tullio Van Zanetti plays a big part in what's going on in this town. I was just wondering if there is anything you know about him or have heard about him on the street or around the department? I think everybody in Philadelphia has heard about Zanetti. I was just thinking if he knows everything that is going on in Philadelphia, just maybe he might know what happened to Paul."

"From what I have heard and know about Zanetti, he is not a cop killer, Tyler replied."

"What do you think about Dan Robinson? Do you think he would know anything about Zanetti he could tell us?"

"I don't know, but when he was Dad's partner, Dad seemed to trust him. He always said he was a good officer."

"How is his wife doing now?"

"Dan comes by the station occasionally, and he just says she has good days and bad days, and when he does come by, he always asks how the investigation is going concerning Dad."

Romo continued the questions. "How about Paul and Eddie? How was their relationship? Did they get along after he married your mother?"

"They all seemed to get along well. Eddie and his wife attended all the police functions. At times, they would sit at the same table with Dad. Then Eddie and his wife separated. She moved back to Baltimore where she was from. About a year after that, Mom and Dad separated. Mom said she and Eddie would meet sometimes and just discuss the situation they were in with their marriages. Dad didn't like that too much. He didn't think she should be discussing their personal lives with anybody else, and I think he went over to the house and told her so. But, you know Mom. I think she told him she would do what the hell she wanted to do because she wasn't married to him anymore. After that, Dad would never speak her name and wouldn't have anything to do with her, other than sign the divorce papers. He never looked back after that. I do think he was a little surprised when he found out she and Eddie were seeing each other."

"Do you think something was going on between Eddie and your mother before their divorce?"

"I don't know, Uncle Romo. I think Dad may have thought so, but if he did, he never mentioned it."

"Do you think he and Eddie ever had any words over it?"

"I don't think so. When Dad and Eddie were in the same room, they were very cordial to each other, but you know Dad. You never knew what he was thinking."

Romo smiled, showing off his deep dimples. He nodded and said, "Yup. That was Paul. How long has Eddie been a motorcycle cop?"

"Ever since he's been a cop. All he has ever wanted to be was a motorcycle cop. He was offered promotions even after he was promoted to sergeant, but he turned them down. He always said he didn't like being in an office, shuffling paperwork. He said he'd rather be outside where he could be with people."

"I can understand that. He didn't seem like the type that would want to be in an office all day. What do you think about Lieutenant Sparrow? Is he known in the department as a good homicide detective?"

"From all I've heard, he's one of the best, and he works hard at being one of the best. Do you think you have something to go on, Uncle Romo, concerning Dad's murderer?"

"Tyler, this is between you and me. I think Paul knew the person that killed him. Paul trusted whoever it was."

With a puzzled look on his face, Tyler exclaimed, "You don't think someone broke in and killed him, do you?"

"I think the murder was set up to look like it was a break-in, but I don't think it was. I'll keep you informed on what I think is going on, but as always, we'll have to keep it confidential."

"I will, Uncle Romo, and if I hear anything, I'll give you a call."

"No, don't do that. I think there's a good possibility my phone is bugged, so if you have anything you want to talk about concerning this case, you need to call and come by. We can take a walk in the park and discuss it."

"I understand. I hadn't thought about it, but there is a good possibility of that."

"I can't believe we've been talking for an hour and forty-five minutes, Tyler. Maybe Sarah might be in a better mood by the time you get home."

"I sure hope so. The last couple weeks she's been hell. I think they're working her too hard at the office."

"Thanks for coming over and talking to me."

"I was glad to do it. If there's anything I can do to help, just give me a call."

As soon as Romo got back into the truck, he went over everything in his mind he and Tyler had discussed. As soon as he walked in the townhouse, he went directly to the trashcan and pulled out the notepad. He turned through a few pages until he got to a clean sheet and started writing each question he had asked Tyler, and the answer Tyler had given. After studying it for a few minutes, he felt like he had it all down. The notebook, beginning with the first page, was going to be where he and Hammy Lee would begin. That thought reminded him he needed to go to the Holiday Inn in the morning and make reservations for Hammy who would be arriving on Saturday. Reservations had to be made in person since he wouldn't be able to use his phone. He put the notebook away and decided to take a shower and go to bed. With all he had running through his mind, he hoped he would be able to sleep. He turned the light off in the kitchen and started down the hall to his bedroom.

~ * ~

The next morning Romo woke early. The digital clock showed that it was four-thirty. He got dressed, and as he was backing out of the driveway, even though it was still dark, he had to be sure he wasn't being followed. When he got to the top of the hill at the stop sign, he needed to turn right, but made a left turn instead. He noticed there were no headlights behind him. He turned into the Bank of America parking lot and stopped. After sitting there for a moment, he pulled out, turned right in the direction to go downtown. Checking his rearview mirror, he felt comfortable that no one was following him. As he was driving through downtown Philadelphia, he noticed that at that time of morning, there appeared to be as many delivery vans and cargo trucks in traffic as there were cars. They were making their morning deliveries to various establishments and businesses. As he approached Seventh Street, he took a left. The Holiday Inn was on the right, and he pulled into customer parking. He looked at his wristwatch... five forty-five. He was hoping to get the reservation made fairly quickly, because he wanted to be sitting at Starbucks at six forty-five. It would be a good opportunity to check out Mr. Zanetti's driver and, maybe, get another good look at Mr. Zanetti.

Romo walked into the high-rise Holiday Inn. A young man was working the front desk. "Good morning," Romo greeted him. "Do you have an availability for two adjoining suites for this coming Saturday through the following week and departing on Sunday morning?"

After taking a couple minutes to look on the computer, the clerk replied, "Yes sir, we do have two suites available for those days. Would you like to reserve them?" Romo nodded yes. "How do you want to pay for this, sir?"

Romo handed him his credit card. "You're paying for both, sir?"

"That's correct. I will be checking in sometime after lunch on Saturday."

The clerk gave Romo a receipt and the room numbers. "We will have two parking spaces available for you, sir, when you check in."

"That's good, young man. You have a good day."

Romo pulled out of the parking lot and headed to Starbucks. When he got there, he parked across the street in front of it. According to his watch, it was six-forty. He was right on time. He got out of the truck and locked the door. As he walked in, it seemed to be a lot smaller than he thought it was going to be. He walked up to the register and ordered a small regular black coffee. After receiving his coffee, he picked up a magazine that was near the newspaper rack and walked over to a table for two in front of the window, which enabled him to watch any vehicle stopping in front of the business. Pleased with the good view, he sat, took a sip of coffee and began thumbing through the magazine.

It was six-fifty and all the regulars started coming in, lining up at the register to place their orders. The coffee shop began to fill up with customers. Some were reading the morning newspapers, some were pulling out papers from their briefcases, and some were exchanging conversation with people at tables and others in line. It was obvious most of them knew each other, perhaps because of their regular visits there.

Checking his watch, he noticed that seven minutes had passed. As soon as he looked back up, a black four-door Mercedes pulled up against the curb right in front of the door. The space was designated as a no parking zone. Sitting in the back seat was a gentleman reading the newspaper. He never looked up. As the car stopped, a man wearing a suit, a white shirt and a necktie got out. He looked as though he might be in his early forties. He had dark hair he had combed straight back. He had a very professional appearance...a very impressive looking man physically. He obviously was a bodybuilder and weightlifter. He had broad shoulders and a thick neck.

He walked up to the register, bypassing everyone in line. He handed the girl behind the register some paper money. She stopped what she was doing and handed him two cups of coffee. He picked up a cup with each hand and walked toward the door. He turned his body sideways, pushing against the door with his hip and shoulder, which caused his suit coat to open wider. Romo could see part of a leather strap that went over his shoulder under the suit. It was evident he was wearing a shoulder holster. He walked around the car, and Zanetti opened the power window and reached through the window for his coffee. The driver then opened the front door on the driver's side of the Mercedes and got in. Romo observed that the door had not been locked. From the slight bit of white smoke coming from the tailpipes of the diesel vehicle, it was obvious he had not even turned off the engine. Most likely this was in order to keep the air-conditioning running. Romo thought to himself that the two men seemed to have no concerns about anybody harming them or causing them any kind of problems whatsoever. It was clear this was a longtime habit, and there was no need to be cautious. Romo smiled to himself, thinking that was a good thing. He folded the magazine, picked up his coffee cup, and walked out.

Romo got into the truck and drove over to the riverfront. The view appeared to be normal, as everyone was working moving freight. As he drove up to the warehouse buildings, he noticed there was a motorcycle cop directing traffic. He was stopping traffic in the right and left lanes, so the tow motors could carry the freight across the street into one of the warehouses. Romo sat and watched. Everything was at a standstill. Finally, the cop motioned for the right lane to come on through. Romo drove by the warehouses slowly. Viewing the inside of one of the warehouses, he saw it was stacked with cargo. As he turned right passing the third warehouse, he noticed the steel roll up doors were closed. There were only two windows facing the street, and they had been blacked out. He slowed down, inspecting the right side of that building. There was approximately a five-foot wide cobblestone walkway going between the buildings. He could not see it, but he thought there must be an entrance door there. After passing the warehouses, he was near the main highway. He headed home and decided he would go for a walk. He had a lot to think about.

~ * ~

Saturday morning finally came. Romo got up early. He made his bed, straightened the house, emptied and cleaned out the refrigerator, and called a taxi. He set his suitcase by the door. While waiting for the taxi, he remembered the gold Cross pen he had found on the floorboard of Paul's truck and had put in the console. He ran to the garage and retrieved the pen which he placed in an envelope and put in his suitcase. He was ready to leave to meet Hammy at the Holiday Inn. A yellow cab finally pulled up in the driveway. Romo placed the door and car keys on the counter. He walked to the front door, picked up his suitcase, and turned the lock on the door knob. He walked out and closed the door, then double checked to be sure it was locked.

It was nine-thirty. Romo told the taxi driver he wanted to go to Hertz car rentals, the one closest to downtown. The driver was wearing a white turban around his head. Romo was not accustomed to seeing that. "Do you speak English?" Romo asked.

The driver looked in the rearview mirror at Romo. "A little bit," he said.

"You did understand the Hertz rental place?"

"Yes, yes, Hertz rental, downtown, yes."

Thirty minutes later, they pulled into the Hertz parking lot. The fare was fifteen dollars. Romo handed the taxi driver a twenty, thanked him, got out, and closed the door.

Romo stepped up to the counter at the rental service, and said to the clerk, "My name's Romo Lindy. I called yesterday for a small cargo van with a sliding door."

"Yes sir, we have it. I'll have it pulled around for you. Just sign right here," he said, placing his finger at the bottom of the paper.

By the time Romo signed and filled out the necessary paperwork, a young man came running inside and handed him the keys. Romo walked over to the van, took the keys, and pushed a button. The door started sliding back. He threw his suitcase in the back and got behind the wheel. He sat for moment just looking around in the vehicle. He mused to himself that there was no front end on the damn thing. It was like sitting on the dashboard looking down, he thought, as he put it in drive and pulled off. As he was driving to center city, he thought he had made a smart choice. About every other vehicle he saw was a white van, so he felt comfortable that he would fit right in.

Sixteen

Romo arrived at the Holiday Inn, parked the van, and went inside where a young woman behind the counter asked if she could help.

"You sure can. I'm Romo Lindy, and I have reservations for two suites on the top floor."

"Yes, sir, all of our suites are on the top floor." She handed him a door key with a green football shaped tag on it.

Romo said, "I think there's supposed to be another one. I had reservations for two suites."

The young lady looked on the computer again. "Yes, sir, you do. I thought somebody might have made a mistake. Both rooms are under one name."

"And the stipulation was that a door from one room opens to the other suite. Is that correct?"

She checked the computer again. "Yes, that's correct."

"I like to have plenty of room when I stay at a hotel," he told her. "Now, I need the key to the other room, if you don't mind."

"Yes sir," she said as she handed him the key. "These are your two parking passes. When you drive in, you will see a box. You have to push the key in it to open the gate. When you get to the very top of the parking deck, there is a door beside the elevator. Open the door with your key, and you will be on the tenth floor. Your rooms will be on the left...ten-oh-four and ten oh-six."

It was five minutes after eleven. Romo decided to go up, find the parking spaces, and take his suitcase to the suite. Then he'd go back down and wait for Hammy Lee. He figured Hammy would be there in about forty-five minutes.

After parking the van, he unlocked the main entrance door, and walked into the hallway. He thought the carpet looked nice, not at all worn. At his room, he opened the door and was impressed. The room had a king-size bed with a television. The main room had two sofas and a recliner, and a small round table with four chairs were in front of the large window. Everything looked relatively new, he thought, as he opened the curtains that covered one side of the room. The room had a good view of the city so he was pleased and hoped Hammy Lee would be, too, since they were definitely going to be there for a few days. He walked over and opened the door to Hammy's room. It was identical to his suite and, like his, everything looked good, and had been taken care of.

Leaving the room, Romo got back on the elevator and stopped on the first floor. As he stepped out, he noticed one door went into the lobby; the other one went outside to the main parking entrance.

He walked to the front entrance and decided to stand outside for a while just in case Hammy showed up earlier than expected. Romo hadn't been waiting but about fifteen minutes when a black four-door Silverado pulled up right in front of him. Romo opened the door.

"How are you doing, Hammy," he said as he stepped up into the truck.

"I'm doing fine, Romo. How are you?"

"I feel better now that you're here. How about backing up a little bit? Pull over in front of the entrance that goes into the parking deck. Here, Hammy. Take this key and put it in that slot. It will raise that arm up." As the arm went up, Hammy pulled inside. He also checked out the exit gate which was on the right side of the entrance gate that could be seen from the lobby.

"Just keep going till you get to the top level."

When they reached the top, Romo said, "Here. Pull up beside this van I rented for us to ride around in."

"Well, it's obvious what you have on your mind, and what we're probably planning on doing."

Romo laughed. "You got me figured out already, Hammy, and we haven't even discussed it."

"Well, you see that kind of stuff on TV all the time. If you're planning on kidnapping someone, you use a van."

Hammy stepped out of the truck. He was wearing overalls and a long-sleeved plaid shirt.

"I see you dressed casual, Hammy."

"If you're going to drive a length of time, you don't need to be wearing pants with a belt, especially if you have a belly like mine. I'm more comfortable this way."

"I understand you have to do what makes you comfortable. I really like that fiberglass cover on the back of this truck. It keeps the rain out, especially if you're hauling something you don't want to get wet."

Hammy let the tailgate down. He had three suitcases. "Those two are yours; this one is mine. Ms. Blackstock wanted to be sure you had enough clothes."

"She knows me. Here, take that key and follow me."

Hammy opened the door to the hallway on the tenth floor. Romo walked a short distance and opened the door to his room. "Just set your suitcase on the floor," Romo said as he went over into Hammy's room. "This is yours."

Hammy walked in, stopped, looked around and exclaimed, "Man! This is nice. I was only expecting one room with a bed."

"I wanted you to have the best."

Hammy walked over and pulled the curtain back. His room also overlooked the city of Philadelphia. "We certainly do have a great view."

"Are you hungry?"

"I could eat a bite."

"I'll call for room service. What would you like?"

"Some kind of sandwich and a cup of coffee will be fine."

Hammy sat in the chair and started taking off his work boots. "Got to let those puppies breathe a little bit. They got a little hot coming up here."

"I understand. Now tell me how things have been going with you now that you're retired."

"Retired? Me and about thirty-three others put in eighteen hours a day. When Dad retired from the hog business, we only had seven people. The best thing I've done was hire myself a good foreman. He's a good old boy out of Randleman, Kenneth Gilly. He graduated from N.C. State with a business degree, so he does all the books. He keeps things out of the red, and he and I work closely. He's a smart man, and he's honest."

"That's good, Hammy."

"Kenneth is the reason I can come up here and spend some time with you. I left him totally in charge, and he won't miss a beat getting things done. I'd bet money on that," Hammy said as he kicked off both boots and lay across the bed.

"I'm going to get you something to read while you're resting." Romo went back to his room, opened his suitcase, pulled out the notepad Paul had left him which also included his own notes. Holding it up in his hand, he walked over beside the bed, and handed it to Hammy.

"This notebook is what Paul left for me in a safety deposit box before he was killed. All the notes of people I have talked to pertaining to this case and their responses are in there, so take your time reading it. You can make some notes on the back side, and we'll discuss it later. Go ahead and get some rest. I'll call you when our sandwiches get here." Romo went back to his room, turned the TV down, and waited for room service.

About twenty minutes later, there was a light knock on his door. A young waiter walked in and set it on the table in front of the window. After tipping the young man, Romo closed the door, and went over, and opened Hammy's door. He was snoring. Romo closed the door and decided he would let him sleep a couple hours before he woke him.

Romo thought he would get a little shut-eye himself, so he kicked off his loafers and lay down on the bed. He woke up to someone knocking on the door. He jumped up and started to answer the door, when he heard the second knock coming from Hammy's room. When he opened it, there stood Hammy. He had unhooked the straps on his overalls and the top part was folded down to his waist. "Damn. What time is it?" Romo said, looking at his watch. "Ten after five. We've been asleep for almost three hours!"

"Well, we must have needed it," replied Hammy.

"I was just going to lie down and rest my eyes," Romo explained.

"You did that for about three hours. They should be rested pretty good by now."

Romo walked over to the table. "Here's our lunch. Come on over and sit."

"You mean dinner, don't you?"

"I guess you could say that."

After eating, they made small talk and exchanged stories about the days when they were police officers with the Greensboro Police Department.

"Okay, let's get down to business. I read everything you had in the notepad, and I've got a few questions for you," Hammy said as he stood. "Excuse me. I've got to do something right quick. I'll be back in a few minutes." Hammy returned from the bathroom holding a plastic cup with toilet tissue crammed in it. He set it on the table, reached in his back pocket and pulled out a plug of Red Man chewing tobacco. He then reached in his pocket, pulled out his pocket knife and cut off a corner piece about the size of a half dollar. He placed it in his mouth with his fingers and worked it into his jaw. The left side of his jaw looked like he had a golf ball in it.

"Now, I'm ready to get down to business," he muttered as he picked up the cup and spit in it. "First question, how did you come to the conclusion that a cop killed Paul?"

Romo took about thirty minutes explaining in detail about the days he and Paul had spent in the boys' school, including all the signs he used to teach him the alphabet.

"Sounds to me like you had a pretty smart brother, Romo."

"There is no doubt he knew I would be here. When I read the letter he wrote, it was obvious somebody was going to try to kill him, and if they succeeded, he knew I would be here."

"After the gun had been stolen, I understand the three officers who had the keys passed lie detector tests."

"That's right. All three passed."

"If that's the case, then it had to be someone close to them who has access to the keys. That means a wife, son, or someone who's close to the family."

"One of the three officers is divorced and has no children. The other is married, and I understand, they are real religious."

"Maybe they need to be checked out first," Hammy said with a laugh.

"And then there's Tyler and his wife Sarah. She works as a paralegal downtown."

"I think the person who has access to the key knows who killed your brother. They may even be working together. It was obvious Paul was getting close to knowing who that was. I think that's the reason he was taken out; he was getting too close. So let's start with the person that has access to that key. To me there is no doubt. Zanetti had it done, and if he didn't, he knows who did. So he is someone we have to get close to. We've got to find out what he knows, and that's going to be tough."

"I'm confident Zanetti knows who did it. As you know, the guy who was tried and turned loose worked for Zanetti."

"Well, if he had the key to get into the warehouse, someone had to give it to him."

"That's true," agreed Romo.

"So, let's start looking for the one with access to the key, and then we'll go for Zanetti to see what he knows."

After discussing the situation for most of the evening, Romo suggested, "Well, it's getting late. Let's sleep on it tonight and talk about it more tomorrow. In the morning after we have breakfast, I'll take you down to the waterfront and give you an update and tell you all I know about Zanetti."

Hammy reached over, spit in his plastic cup, and answered, "That sounds good to me."

"You know you have a coffee pot in your room, don't you?"

"Yes. I saw it when I got my cup. Let's have coffee around seven o'clock," Hammy suggested as he picked up his plastic cup and walked back into his room."

Romo picked up the phone and dialed the front desk and asked for a six a.m. wake up call. Having taken care of that, he sat on the side of the bed thinking about the conversation they just had and where to start in the morning. He would get Hammy's ideas on that.

~ * ~

The next morning at seven, there was a light knock on Romo's door. "Come on in, Hammy. You're just in time. Room service just brought our breakfast."

Hammy walked in wearing his carpenter jeans with a hammer loop on the side and a brown and tan checked, long-sleeved shirt. He looked neat with his graying, dark, naturally curly hair that had just been shampooed. He sat at the table in front of the window and lifted the metal cover off the plate. "Man, that looks good."

"No grits. They only had hashbrowns."

"That's fine. I can eat them, too."

"I was just thinking. As soon as we get through with breakfast, we'll take the van and drive down to the waterfront. There are a few things I'd like to show you," Romo said.

"Sounds good to me. I'd like to see this town, anyway.

Seventeen

As they entered the waterfront area, Hammy remarked, "It looks like some of those buildings go back a long ways."

"I was told some of them go back to the late 1700s and early 1800s."

As they turned into the waterfront area, Hammy observed, "Well, it's not much traffic out this morning. Looks like everybody is getting ready to go to church."

Romo pointed to a building, and said, "Those two belong to Zanetti. He uses them for storage and makes the customers pay double. Zanetti sees to it that they are used whether they need to be or not. He's making a killing. The union knows it and supports him." Romo drove up a little further and turned right. He stopped in front of a two-story building. "This building is also Zanetti's. I think there may be an entrance up that alley," he explained, pointing in the direction where a small cobblestone walkway went beside the building.

Romo had slowed to a stop. Hammy opened the door. "Hold on a minute. I'll take a look." It seemed to Romo that he was gone for about thirty minutes when just at that time, he saw Hammy walking out of the alley. Romo asked, "Is there a door on that side?"

"Yep," Hammy answered. "It had the old skeleton key lock so I just took my credit card and opened it and went in. The floors are that old tongue and groove wood. I wouldn't be afraid to bet they are the original floors in that building. About a third of it has caved in."

Romo added, "That's why they're not using it."

Hammy continued describing what he had seen. "They have a hook and a chain that's on a pulley. I suppose they used it to hoist up bales of cotton or some kind of cargo. It's on a metal rail, and it slides back and forth. There are some old empty boxes, some wooden pallets, a few empty metal barrels, and a couple of cinderblocks, and that's about it. Those two doors that enter from the road are kept closed by an old metal bar that's laid across two metal hooks."

Romo said, "I have a couple more places I want to show you." He turned right and went up the road a couple of blocks, turned left, pulled up to the stop sign, and stopped. Romo pointed across the street, and said, "See that Starbucks? Zanetti and his driver and bodyguard stop there every morning around seven. Zanetti sits in the car while the bodyguard goes in and gets two cups of coffee which are waiting for him on the counter. The guy goes right in, throws a greenback on the counter, picks up the coffee, and walks right back out. He leaves the car idling so the air-conditioning will keep running."

Hammy replied, "That's very interesting. Zanetti must feel pretty safe for his bodyguard to do that."

"Oh, yes. He thinks he's untouchable."

"Well, that's a good thing for us."

Romo looked over at Hammy, knowing he and Hammy were thinking the same thing. "Got one other place I need to show you. It's a little ways out of town. I think you're going to like it."

"Let's get to it. There's nothing like a nice Sunday morning drive."

Romo drove for about thirty minutes. He pulled up between the two brick columns at the entrance to the Philadelphia Country Club.

"Who lives out here?" Hammy inquired.

Romo pointed, and said, "See that house up there? That's Zanetti's."

"Man! That's one hell of a house."

"And I understand it's just he and his wife who live there." As Romo went around a curve, he pointed at the next house. "Now, that's his girlfriend's house, and that lot backs right up to Zanetti's lot. So if he gets pissed off at his wife, he can just walk across the yard right into the back door of his girlfriend's house."

"Man. He's got balls as big as grapefruits to do something like that."

"His wife may not know about her, and probably doesn't care as long as she gets what she wants."

"Sounds like he has it made, Romo. How old is this guy?"

"He's about fifty to fifty-five. Seems he's in pretty good health, too. I think we better get out of this neighborhood and head back. Two old white guys riding around in a white van in this neighborhood may not go over too well."

As they got back on the highway, Romo said, "Okay. I'm going to show you one other place that started this whole mess. It's on the highway going back to the hotel." As they started back into the city, Romo turned on Commerce St.

"That brick building on the right is the new warehouse." Hammy looked at it. "It sure doesn't look like a warehouse to me. I wasn't expecting this type of building."

Mo said, "That's what the department likes about this place. There's no doubt about it. There has to be someone working on the inside who's involved, and that's what we have to figure out. Well it's getting late. We can have dinner and talk more about it at the hotel."

"Sounds good to me," Hammy said as Romo turned toward the hotel.

After arriving, they went in, and ordered room service. Later, they fixed themselves drinks using the bourbon out of the mini-bars they had in their rooms. They sat at the round table in front of the windows overlooking the city.

Hammy turned to Romo, and said, "I think I know what you have on your mind, Mo. I have thought about it, and that may be our only way to get the information we need to find out who killed Paul, and who's breaking into the warehouse."

"What are you thinking, Hammy?"

"I'm thinking we're going to have to kidnap Zanetti, and take him somewhere, and figure out a way to make him talk. I've got a feeling that's going to be hard. It's not going to be easy to get that man to spill the beans."

Romo looked at Hammy with a big grin. "I think that's something we both have got to think about and figure out how we are going to do it without getting caught or killed."

"What I would like to do, Mo, is this: "You and I go down to Starbucks in the morning. I'd like to get a good look at Zanetti and his driver. We need to start looking at this seriously. Let's get up in the morning early and drive down, and be there before seven."

"That sounds good to me. I'll have room service at five-thirty. We'll eat a bite before we leave."

"We need to be there at least ten to fifteen minutes before they arrive."

"I agree with that."

Hammy stood up to leave. "Sounds good to me. I'll see you in the morning."

~ * ~

Romo heard Hammy pecking on his door.

"Come on in," Romo yelled from the table. "You're just in time. Room service just left. Have a seat."

Hammy sat and took the silver cover off his plate which boasted scrambled eggs, bacon and hashbrowns. "They probably don't have homemade biscuits and gravy or grits."

"You have a choice between bacon or sausage. I've tried the sausage, so bacon would be your best choice. We should probably hurry up things a little. It's a little after six. We should get going as soon as we can, because you never know about the traffic up here."

~ * ~

They pulled up in front of Starbucks, parked across the street, got out of their van, and walked into the store. Romo said, "I'll get the coffee. You find us a seat in front of the window." After getting the coffee, Romo joined Hammy, where they could face the street.

At seven on the dot, the black Mercedes pulled in front. The driver got out and went inside. Hammy looked at his watch. The driver walked over, laid some folded money on the counter, and picked up to two coffees that had already been made for him. As he walked toward the door holding a cup of coffee in each hand, he used his hip to open the door, walked around to the back of the Mercedes, and handed Zanetti his coffee through the window. He got back in the driver's seat and pulled away.

Hammy said, "It only took him twenty-five seconds to come in, and get the coffee, and get back outside. He left the car running, which means he left the keys in the car. He's a pretty big fella. He looks like a body builder. His shirt collar looks like it should be about a size twenty-two."

"Every bit of it. Hammy. I wonder if he's wearing a bulletproof vest under that suit."

"If he's not, he's a big boy," Hammy replied. "I didn't get a good look at Zanetti. He had that newspaper half in his face. I tell you what, Romo. Let's drive down to the waterfront and this time see how long it takes to get down there." They got into the van and made a U-turn in the middle of the road. Mo drove towards the waterfront. With the traffic, it only took four and a half minutes to get to the waterfront.

Hammy suggested they go back to the hotel and discuss the situation. They didn't have much to say as they drove. They were both deep in thought.

Hammy broke the silence. "Mo, do you know where a Lowe's is located?"

"Yep, there's one not far from here."

"Well, let's go there. I need to pick up a few things."

Romo didn't question him. "We're on our way. Should be there in about fifteen minutes."

As they entered Lowe's, Hammy asked one of the service clerks, "Where are your gas grills?" The clerk pointed and gave directions.

"Thank you," Hammy said as he walked in that direction. He stopped and looked around. "That's it," he said as he approached a turkey cooker. "This is the one I want, but I don't need the pot that's setting on it."

The clerk responded, "I can sell it to you for twenty-five dollars if you don't want the pot."

"That's good. We'll take it. Now, do you have any filled gas tanks?"

"Yes, sir. They are over there against that wall," he said, pointing. Romo picked up a gas tank, and they walked to the register.

Hammy asked the clerk where he could get a few gallons of water. Romo looked at Hammy but never said a word. Hammy continued, "We need to get twenty-five gallon jugs of water." Romo still remained silent. He grabbed a flat pushcart, and they loaded up the containers of water. They checked out and started toward the van. "What are we going to do with all this water?"

"I've got a plan, Mo. I'll explain when we get in the van."

Eighteen

Once in the van, Hammy said, "Okay, Romo. This is my plan. We go to the waterfront about six o'clock." We need to go down to that old warehouse, the one we looked at yesterday. I'll go to the side door and open it, then I'll open the double doors for you to drive in. Once we get inside, I'll take one of the barrels and two cinderblocks that are already in there and set them up right under the rail that has that sliding hook on it. I'm going to set the barrel on top of the cinderblocks, and then I'm going to slide this burner right under the middle of it. I'm going to pour the twenty-five gallons of water in it. We'll get Zanetti in there and put him on the hook. Then the water will come to a boil just like when you're skinning pigs. You know you have to get the hair off them before you can start cutting them up."

Romo's eyes went wide. "You're not going to scald him, are you, Hammy?"

"No, but he's not going to know that. I'm just going to lower him down close to the boiling water, feet first. I think by the time he feels the heat, he'll tell you anything you want to know."

"That's something I haven't thought about."

"Well, this guy's not going to talk if we threaten him or slap him around a little bit. So I think we've got to go to a little more extreme and make him think we're going to do it."

"It certainly is extreme, but I think you're right. Slapping him around is not going to make him talk."

"I think we need to go back down in the morning and make a practice run from Starbucks to warehouse number three. We'll time how long the bodyguard is inside one more time and see how long it takes him to be back out. Then we'll time how long it takes us to get to the warehouse. You know all hell's going to break loose because everybody is going to be looking for him, including the police department. So, we need to get him in the warehouse, get the information we need from him and get the hell out. I don't see why we can't do it. They do this kind of stuff in the movies and on TV all the time."

"You're right, Hammy. The only difference is, they're going to have real guns with real bullets."

"I think we can do it. We've just got to be fast at it, that's all. When we get back to our rooms we'll discuss it further. I do think we need to do it this week, maybe Wednesday or Thursday. We don't have that much time to set things in motion."

As soon as they walked back into Romo's room, they went straight to the minibar. Romo looked at his watch. "It's not even noon yet, Hammy, and we're starting to drink."

"I've been up since four o'clock, so it's afternoon for me. Let's sit over here at the table and start writing down what we need, just to be sure."

Romo pulled out the drawer and got out a writing pad with the Holiday Inn logo at the right top corner. Hammy dictated: "The first thing on the agenda should be duct tape, at least two rolls. Next, we need something to pull over his head."

"I'll take the pillow case off of the bed," Romo offered.

Hammy continued, "We'll need two flashlights."

As Romo was writing, Hammy said, "I think I have two flashlights in my truck. I also have a cigarette lighter. We definitely need that to light the burner. And it wouldn't hurt if we had a couple pair of gloves to wear," he added as Romo continued writing. They sat for few minutes thinking about the things they needed. Neither said a word. Then, Hammy had a sudden thought, "Oh, and let's not forget the cassette recorder."

"I've got one with new batteries in it," Romo said.

"I've got one too," Hammy added. "We'll take both of them just in case one fails. That's a must. I want to have everything he says on tape."

They agreed they had probably thought of everything but wanted to go over the list and the plan again, just to be certain what they were going to do, and when they were going to do it. They took a swallow of their mixed drinks and began their task. Romo suggested they start from the beginning, from the time they left the hotel until they got in position.

Hammy said, "I think we need to leave here about five-thirty to drive to the warehouse. I'll go in the side door, take the bar off and open the doors for you to drive in. I think we need to go ahead and set up everything while we're there. I'll grab two cinderblocks and set the barrel on them. Then, we'll put the burner under the barrel so we'll have that much ready to go. And it might be a good idea to go ahead and put the twenty-five gallons of water in it. If we do that, all we'll have to do is light the burner."

"I think we need to light the burner before we leave, so it will be ready when we get back," Romo suggested.

"You're right. It will save time. And before we leave, we'll take a piece of duct tape and tape those double doors together. That way, I'll only have to take the van and push against it and it will come open easily. I'll jump out and put the bar back across the double doors."

"All that sounds good to me, Hammy. Once we get to Starbucks, we'll park the van on the same side of the street the bodyguard parks the Mercedes, but about two car lengths behind him. As soon as he steps out of his car, you need to start the van. Once he opens the door to go into Starbucks, you will need to drive out and pull up beside the Mercedes with the sliding door open. I will jump out, open Zanetti's door, grab him and throw him headfirst through the open door of the van with me on top of him. As soon as I do that, you need to be pulling out, and then hit the button for the sliding door to close. I'll handcuff him and put a piece of duct tape over his mouth and slide the pillowcase over his head. Then, I'll wrap a few rounds of duct tape around his ankles. Hopefully, we'll be out of sight by the time the bodyguard comes out."

"So far all of that sounds good," Hammy said. "Now, in the morning, we need to go through this one more time from the beginning. We'll drive to Starbucks and stop exactly where we think we'll need to be. Again, we'll count the seconds the bodyguard is gone. Then, we'll drive to the warehouse and count that time as well." Romo turned up his glass, swallowed the last of his drink, and commented, "That all sounds good to me, Hammy."

~ * ~

The next morning. Hammy and Romo got up early and implemented their plan. They were sitting on the right side of the road near the curb at Starbucks, but back far enough to give Zanetti's bodyguard room to pull in and stop. Romo checked the time. "Well, it's about six fifty-five. They should be here about anytime."

Romo turned facing Hammy and admitted, "This is the first time I've broken the law in any way."

"Yeah, this is my first time, too, Romo, but I always felt like if I was going to break the law, I would do a good job at it."

Romo couldn't help but grin as he shook his head slightly.

"Four minutes after seven. They're running late, Romo." Hammy had no more gotten the words out of his mouth when the black Mercedes pulled up. When the bodyguard got out of the vehicle, Hammy and Romo started timing him the minute he opened the door to Starbucks. Nineteen seconds had gone by when he walked back out.

"Well, he did it quicker this time. Twenty-five seconds was what it had taken before. Six seconds faster this time. Romo pulled out of the parking space and started down to the waterfront. Hammy checked his watch. After Romo made his turn and pulled up in front of the warehouse, Hammy said, "That took five minutes exactly, and we had very little traffic. We can do this. I think when we pull up beside him, and you open the door and grab him, he will be in so much shock he won't even put up a fight. After you pull him out, throw him in the back of the van and hold him down, I'm pretty sure you won't have a problem handcuffing him. Let's go by Lowe's, and pick up the duct tape, and the other things we need. We'll go back to the hotel, and lay everything out, and go over everything one more time. I think we need to go ahead with it in the morning."

"I'm ready," Romo said.

After buying duct tape, two pair of gloves, and an additional cigarette lighter at Lowe's, Romo said, "I went ahead and picked up some flashlight batteries, just to make sure the ones in my flashlights haven't run down." As they were about to leave the store, Romo noticed a plastic tarp, nine by twelve in size, and said, "I think I'm going to get this to lay down in the back of the van just in case he gets a bloody nose or something; it'll keep the van clean." Hammy agreed. "That'll be good. We don't want to leave any evidence."

As Romo was about to pull out of Lowe's parking lot, his phone rang. He looked to see who was calling. "I ought to answer this. It's Tyler, Paul's son."

"Is he the one that's with the police department?"

Romo nodded.

"Hi, Uncle Romo. I've been calling the house and couldn't get an answer."

"I've been pretty busy, Tyler. What can I do for you?"

"Well, all hell has broken loose here."

"What do you mean?"

"Over the weekend, somebody used a key and went inside the warehouse, and took the two hundred packages of cocaine. They replaced it with two hundred packages of small bags of flour wrapped in plastic and duct tape. They tried to make it look like the packages that were already there, hoping no one would notice the difference. This was discovered when I took a DEA agent over there this morning. The agent wanted to check on the shipment. When he picked up a package, it seemed heavier than it should have been, so he took out his knife, and stuck it in the package. It turned out to be flour. All the detectives are over there investigating. The lieutenant has taken the key from me and has gone to find the other two fellows to take their keys as well. It's going to be hell around here for a few days. I can't say when you and I will have a chance to talk again, but I will be talking to you as soon as I get the time."

Romo asked, "Aren't there security cameras?"

"We were in the process of installing them, so whoever went in there knew we didn't have the cameras working yet.

"I understand, Tyler. You be careful. I'll talk to you later."

Romo looked at Hammy and said, "This is not going to be good for us. Over the weekend, someone used a key and went into the new location where they had stored two hundred packages of cocaine and took them without leaving any kind of evidence. Investigators have taken the key away from Tyler and are on the way over to get the keys from the other two guys. So, as of today, they'll probably be keeping a close eye on Zanetti, which means we've got to be extra careful in the morning. They could have someone watching him at the same time we're planning to try to pick him up, so that means we've got to keep a lookout for the DEA agents as well as the Philadelphia Police Department."

"Boy, this is really getting exciting, isn't it, Romo?"

"Yes, it is, but I think we've gone too far to back out now."

"Yep," Hammy agreed.

Romo continued, "Let's go back to the room and lay everything out one more time. And let's get off the highway. I've got a feeling there will be cops everywhere by this afternoon."

"And I hope not in the morning. We need to check everything out carefully before we make our move."

Nineteen

The next morning Romo and Hammy were up at four-thirty. Hammy walked into Romo's room wearing his overalls with suspenders, a cotton tan and black checked shirt, and his work boots. "It looks like you're going to work on the hog farm this morning, Hammy."

"I do my best work wearing these clothes, and I need to be at my best today."

"You can say that again, old buddy. I think I have everything we're going to need."

As they started toward the door, Hammy said, "Hold on a minute." He ran into the bathroom and came back holding a plastic cup with toilet tissue stuffed in it. "I'm ready now. Let's go. When we get all of this to the van, we'll check it all out, and lay that tarp down in the back. We probably need to tape it down before we get there to keep it from sliding around."

When they pulled out of the parking deck, Romo checked the time. It was five twenty-five. "We'll be there in about twenty minutes. That should give us time to set everything up in the warehouse, shouldn't it, Hammy?"

"Yes, and from there, we're not but five minutes away from Starbucks, so we should have plenty of time." Not a word was spoken between them as they drove along. They were keeping their thoughts to themselves.

Just before Romo pulled up to the double doors of the warehouse, he turned off his headlights. Hammy grabbed a flashlight, jumped out and went around the side and up the cobblestone walkway without turning his flashlight on until he reached the door. In just a few minutes, the double door opened and Romo pulled inside. By the time Romo had taken the gas burner out of the van, Hammy had two cinderblocks on the floor. "Romo, help me with the barrel."

After setting the barrel on the cinderblocks under the steel rail that had the chain and hook on it, Hammy slid the burner under the barrel and hooked up the gas. He lit the burner, and it started right up. He adjusted the flame. "Man, I hope this place doesn't burn down before we get back," Hammy said.

"I hope not, too. We'll be in one hell of a shape if it does."

"But if we don't start the burner now, we'll be here too long waiting for the water to heat up. Now start taking the caps off those gallon jugs of water. I'll start pouring them in the barrel."

After that was done, Romo looked at his watch: six twenty-five. "Let's just take our time and drive up to Starbucks."

Romo backed out with his lights off. Hammy took the duct tape, closed the double doors, and taped them together from the inside. When Hammy came out, Romo had moved to the passenger seat. As Hammy got in the driver's seat, he assured Romo, "Those doors shouldn't be a problem to open. It will only take a slight bump with the van. After I pull in, I'll close the doors and put the steel bar back."

"Just like we planned," Romo said. "We've got plenty of time. Let's just take our time getting there."

"You got it, buddy," Hammy replied as he turned right on the riverfront and drove toward Starbucks. Hammy drove slowly past Starbucks. Then he made a U-turn and pulled over to the curb about four car lengths back from where Zanetti's bodyguard usually pulled in.

Romo reached in the back of the van behind the driver's seat and pulled out a roll of duct tape. "What are you going to do with that, Romo?"

"I'm just going to pull off a couple small strips and tack it on the back of the seat here. In case he starts hollering like a little girl, I'm going to put the tape over his mouth, then I'm going to handcuff him. Just hope nothing goes wrong."

"It's about five minutes until seven. You better get ready," Hammy warned.

Romo got out and opened the sliding door, leaving it open as he got back in. "Okay, I'm set. By the way, if things go wrong, I want you to go back to the hotel, clean out your room, and get the hell back to North Carolina as fast as you can. I've fixed it so there is no evidence of you ever being here. Everything is in my name."

"Nothing is going to go wrong, big guy. You just throw his ass in the back. I'll take care of the rest." Hammy reached in his back pocket and pulled out a plug of Red Man. Rather than taking his pocket knife and cutting off a piece of it, he just stuck in his mouth, bit off a big mouthful, and slid it all to one side of his jaw.

"Now, don't forget to push the sliding door button once we get in. I sure would hate to be going down the road and fall out of the van. Wouldn't that be a hell of a sight?" Romo said.

Looking in his rearview mirror, Hammy yelled, "Here he comes, Romo. It's showtime!"

The black Mercedes pulled up in front of them and stopped near the curb. "Okay, get ready."

"I'm ready. Let's do it."

Hammy started the van. Once the bodyguard opened the door to go into Starbucks, Hammy pulled up beside the Mercedes. Romo jumped out and opened the back door of the Mercedes. Zanetti leaned over in the seat with a terrified look on his face. Romo grabbed Zanetti by his suit jacket and jerked him out. He took one step toward the van and threw him through the open door. Without his feet even touching the road, Romo sailed on top of Zanettti. When Hammy felt the bounce of the van, he pulled out, and pushed the button to close the door.

Zanetti lay still. Romo had knocked the breath out of him. Before Zanetti could get his breath, Romo had him handcuffed. Hammy looked in the rearview mirror. The bodyguard had not come out. "We're in the clear," he said without calling Romo's name.

Because he wasn't able to catch his breath, Zanetti was not able to put up a fight. Romo felt a gun in the holster Zanetti had on under his suit coat. "Here, hold on to this," Romo shouted as he handed the gun up front to Hammy.

As soon as Zanetti could speak, the first thing he said was, "Get off me, you son of a bitch. I think you broke my ribs." Romo taped his mouth shut.

Hammy made a left turn and pulled up in front of the warehouse. He pushed against the doors with the front of the van. They swung wide open as he pulled inside. He put the van in park and turned the engine off. He jumped out and ran back, closed the doors, and placed the metal bar across them.

They pulled Zanetti out of the van. Romo had already put the pillowcase over his head and taped his ankles. Zanetti tried to speak but with the tape across his mouth, he sounded like someone trying to talk underwater. They lugged him over to a stack of wooden pallets that had been piled up near the barrel and sat him down. Hammy bent over close to Zanetti's face. "I'm going to pull the tape off your mouth, but if you make the slight bit of noise, I'm going to take this gun and shut your mouth with it. Do you understand what I'm telling you, Zanetti?"

Zanetti nodded his head vigorously. Hammy reached up under the pillowcase and jerked off the tape, leaving the shroud over his head. Hammy and Romo picked Zanetti up by his arms and dragged him over to where the hook and chain were hanging. Hammy placed the hook between the handcuffs and pulled Zanetti's arms up over his head. Zanetti began to talk. "Do you sons of bitches know who you're dealing with here? I will have both of your asses for this!"

Hammy answered sharply. "Just look who the hell is threatening who, especially someone who might not ever see daylight again." Hammy went over and took the shoes off his captive's feet, and cut the tape from around his ankles. He then unbuckled Zanetti's belt and slid his pants down to his ankles. Hammy pulled them off and threw them on the pallets stacked nearby.

"What the hell are you doing," Zanetti shouted.

Romo raised him up off the floor with the hook and chain while Hammy taped his ankles together again. "What do you guys want? Money? If that's what you're after, I've got money. I will pay you more than whoever it is that's paying you to do this."

"We're not after money, Zanetti. We're after information."

"Who are you anyway? With that damn accent, I know you're not from around here."

"You're right about that, Zanetti."

"What kind of information are you looking for?"

"To start off with, we want to know who killed Paul Riggs."

"Who in the hell is Paul Riggs?"

"He was an Internal Affairs Officer with the Philadelphia Police Department. He was murdered about three weeks ago."

"I have no idea who in the hell did that job."

"Well, we'll see about that," Romo said as he started raising Zanetti off the floor with the chain and hook. Hammy guided Zanetti over to the top of the barrel and said, "Where I come from, the way you get hair off a hog is to boil him first. We're going to boil the meat off your feet and keep moving up from there until you tell us what we want to know."

Zanetti could feel the heat from the boiling water on the bottom of his feet. Hammy continued explaining. "In case you didn't hear me the first time, where we come from this is what we do to hogs. We're going to put your feet in this boiling water until the meat on your feet and legs come off the bones."

Zanetti's voice was quivering, and he was having a hard time getting a full sentence out. "Wait a minute, wait a minute," he said as he felt it getting hotter. "I'll tell you, if you'll move me off the top of this boiling water. My feet are getting too hot."

"And they're going to get hotter than that if you don't start talking," Hammy warned.

Zanetti replied, "I think Riggs was getting close to knowing who went into the warehouse and exchanged the gun. I told a cop about it."

"Who was the cop?" Romo inquired.

"He's been on my payroll for two and a half years."

"What's his name?"

Zanetti was quiet for a minute. "I can't tell you that."

Hammy acted quickly. He grabbed Zanetti at his waist and started moving him closer to the barrel. "Okay, okay, okay! His first name is Eddie and I don't remember his last name."

"Would his last name be Reynolds?" Romo asked.

"Yeah. That's it! That's it! Reynolds. Eddie Reynolds. He's a motorcycle cop."

"How did you get the key to open the gate and the door?"

Again, Zanetti got quiet.

"Don't make me have to ask you again," Romo warned him.

"There's a cop on first shift that has a key. We gave his wife a mold block so she could make an imprint of the key."

Hammy looked at Romo, knowing what he was thinking by the expression on his face. Romo put his hand on his forehead and looked down, wiping his hand across his face, back and forth so hard that when he took it away, his face was blood red. Hammy hadn't seen that expression on Romo's face in the twelve years he had known him.

"Is she Tyler Riggs' wife?"

"I don't know her husband's name. I just know he's a cop and works first shift, and he's the one who had the key to the warehouse. But I don't think he knew anything about it. All I know is we paid his wife ten grand to get that key print, and then we had the key made from it. Eddie had a van made up with the same decals on it as the Philadelphia Police

Department, so he just opened the gate and the doors, went in with the van, got the gun, and came back out."

"Is he the one who took the van and went in, and got the two hundred bags of cocaine over the weekend?"

"Are you guys cops? How did you know about that?"

Hammy spoke up. "We know a lot, Zanetti, and we'll know if you're telling the truth, and if you're not, you're going in that damn boiling water. Do you hear me? Where did you take the cocaine?"

"Eddie got it Sunday night. He took it to Jersey City and put it in a warehouse over there."

"In Jersey City? Where in Jersey City?"

"It's on MacArthur Street across from a Pizza Hut."

"Zanetti, I think you've told us the truth, so I'm going to do you a favor," Romo said. "I've made a recording of everything you've told us. When we leave here, I'm going to put the cassette tape in an envelope, and I'm going to mail it to the John Gotti family in New York. They should get it in about two days, three days at the most. So, this is the time when you need to go home, get your wife or girlfriend or both, get what money you've got stashed away, and see how far away you can get from Philadelphia."

"You know damn well I won't last long once you do that."

"That depends on how far you can go, and how easily you can disappear." Romo looked at Hammy and motioned for him to get the gas burner and put it in the van. It was time to clean up and get going. Hammy put all the empty gallon water jugs in the van and cleaned up all traces of their presence. He then walked over and kicked over the barrel of boiling water. He took the handcuffs off Zanetti, put his hands in front of him, and wrapped his wrists together with duct tape.

Romo took the belt out of Zanetti's pants loops and put it around Zanetti's waist. He reached up and got the hook on the end of the chain and attached it to Zanetti's belt. He pulled it up just tight enough to keep Zanetti in place. "Okay, Zanetti. We're going to leave now. By the time you take your teeth and pull the tape from around your hands, it won't take you long to be out of here and on your way, and we will be on our way out of town. Thanks for the info."

Hammy opened the warehouse doors and pulled the van outside, then stopped, closed the doors, hopped back in the van, and drove off. He drove the speed limit all the way back to the hotel, noticing that there were police cars going in both directions. Before pulling into the Holiday Inn parking area, they went around to the back. Romo gathered up their materials: the plastic with the gas burner, gas tank, empty containers, and threw them all in a dumpster. He got back in the van, and said, "I think it will be empty by Friday."

Twenty

"Where are we going now?" Hammy inquired.

"I want to take this van back and lease a car. The quicker I get this thing off my hands. the better I'll feel."

After turning in the van, Romo leased a white Dodge Intrepid. "This one rides a little better, doesn't it, Hammy?"

"It sure does. I like looking over the hood of a car and not straight down on the road like that damn van. What's the next move now?"

"I want to go back to the room and just sit and listen to that tape again, and see if we can put it all together."

"That sounds like a good idea to me."

Thinking back on what they had just experienced, Romo shared his thoughts. "I think it's obvious Eddie was the one who killed Paul. He was the cop Paul was trying to tell me did it. But what really surprised me was Sarah."

"Sarah?"

"That's Tyler's wife."

"Oh, yes. I remember now. I wonder if Tyler knew anything about it."

"I don't think so," Romo answered as he pulled into the entrance of the parking deck. "He passed all the lie detector tests." Romo said, "I know it's only ten-fifteen. Do you think it's too early to have a drink, Hammy?"

"Hell, no. After what we've just been through, any man would need a drink right now."

They went straight to their rooms. With a big sigh, Romo said, "Man, I am glad that's over." He laid the cassette tapes on the table and went over to the mini-bar.

"I think I'm going to have me a double," Hammy said.

"Me, too," Romo replied while fixing their drinks. "Can you believe what we've just done?"

"Yep, and I loved it."

Romo couldn't help but laugh at his remark. "What do we do now?"

"Well I've got one or two ideas, but I haven't figured out which one I want to do first. I need to think about it for a few minutes. What I would like to do is get in my car and go find Eddie and do to him what he did to my brother. But I know Paul wouldn't like that at all, and he wouldn't want me to do it. So, I think I'll call the lieutenant and let him take care of all of this. And I probably need to call him right away and tell him where the cocaine is located, that is, if they haven't moved it by now."

Romo pulled out his wallet and took out the business card Lieutenant Sparrow had given him. He picked up the house phone and called the number on the card. Surprisingly, he got an immediate answer.

"How are you, Lieutenant? This is Romo."

"Where in the hell have you been? I've been calling the townhouse for you."

"Just give me a minute. Are you sitting down?"

"No, I'm not sitting down."

"Well, find a chair. I've got something to tell you that you'll need to write down."

"Okay, I've got pencil. Go ahead."

Twenty-one

"The cocaine that was stolen from your warehouse is in a Jersey City warehouse on MacArthur Street. It's right across the street from a Pizza Hut. That's where it was taken Sunday night. So you need to get a move on it quickly before they take it to New York."

"Are you sure about this, Romo?"

"Well, Zanetti volunteered this information to me and, at the time, I don't think he was lying."

"So you are the one who kidnapped him."

"Let's just say I detained him for a little while."

Sparrow answered, "I'll call you back later tonight. Let me get on this," and he hung up.

"Okay, Hammy. He's moving on it. I sure hope they get there in time."

"I'm going to fix another drink. You want one?"

"Yes, I think I will have another."

"Well, all we can do now is sit and wait for him to call you back."

"I've got a feeling that if he calls back, it will be sometime tonight around nine or ten."

"A lot depends on what they find in that warehouse."

"I'm thinking about asking him to come over here and let him listen to the tape for himself. That way he'll hear it first hand and will know that what I'm telling him is a fact."

"That's true. How do you think he's going to take what we did to get that information?"

"I don't know. Maybe I'll ask for an informant confidentiality and see what he thinks of that. It's seven o'clock. If you don't mind, I think I'll ride over to a friend's house. If the lieutenant calls while I'm gone, just tell him I'll call him back. I'll only be gone for about an hour to an hour and a half."

"Sure, go ahead. I think I'm going to take a nap. Just knock on my door when you come back in case I'm asleep."

"I think I'll take the tape and listen to it as I'm driving."

"You might as well take the other one too; one could be easier to understand than the other."

"That's a good idea. I'll take them both." He picked up the recorders. He also picked up his 44 Magnum and put it in his shoulder holster under his jacket.

As Romo pulled out of the parking deck, he reached over and activated one of the cassette tapes and listened to it for about thirty minutes. By then, he had arrived at Jessie's. He pulled into the driveway, but before he could get out, another car pulled up behind him. He checked it out in the rearview mirror; it was Gene.

Gene walked up to the driver's side of the vehicle. "Hey there, Gene. I thought you were having surgery on your eye."

"Had to put it off for a couple more weeks. The reason I'm here is not good news for you, Romo. Every mob figure on the waterfront is out looking for you and your partner. They're out now checking on all the hotels and motels in Philadelphia for two men with southern accents. They're scouring all the parking lots and parking decks for any vehicles with tags from the south. They're also calling desk clerks and asking for anyone who has registered with a deep southern accent."

Romo raised his eyebrows and listened intently to hear what Gene might have further to say. "The word on the street is Zanetti told his underboss what happened, and then he went home, got his wife and left town. Nobody has any idea where he went. As of right now, he can't be found."

Romo reached in the passenger seat and handed Gene the two tape recorders.

"Give these to Lieutenant Sparrow and move your car. I've got to get back to the hotel." When Romo left and made the turn out of the complex, the tires were squealing. He had a feeling the people looking for them might find Hammy asleep, and Hammy would open the door, not knowing who they were. When Romo got to the parking deck, he noticed Hammy's truck was still in its space. Just maybe they haven't gotten here, he thought, as he walked up to the door.

He stopped and listened to see if there was any sound coming from his room. Not hearing any, he opened the door. Looking around, he knew there had been one hell of a fight. The round table had been turned over, the television knocked off its stand, and both lamps were lying on the floor. He looked into Hammy's room. It had also been ransacked. They were searching for the tapes, he thought.

The first place Romo thought of looking for Hammy was the Four Jokers. Romo left hastily and ran to his vehicle, pulled out of the parking deck, and headed for the waterfront. It seemed like it took forever to get there. When he arrived, there was a parking space just below the bar.

He parked, took a deep breath, walked in, and looked around. He noticed a staircase going up the side of the wall near the bar. He started walking toward the stairs. When he got to the bottom of the steps, he saw a huge man wearing a white shirt and black tie standing there. Romo figured he was the enforcer. The big man stepped in front of Romo as he started up the steps. Romo hit him in the throat. The guy fell backwards against the wall, holding his throat with his mouth and eyes wide open.

Romo ran up the steps. At the first door he came to, he stopped and listened. There was no sound coming from the inside. He walked on down the hall. He could hear noises coming from the next door before he got there. Romo backed up against the other side of the wall, stepped forward and kicked open the door open. There sat Hammy in a chair tied up with ropes from his neck down to his feet. Blood was running from the side of his head and mouth, and his head hung down. Romo flew into a rage. There were three men standing around Hammy. Romo recognized one of them as Zanetti's bodyguard, Jimmy Sisko. All three appeared to be in shock when they saw Romo. All the self-defense training Romo had received in the Navy Seals automatically sprang into action. Before anybody could move, Romo hit the bodyguard first with his fist, sending him down to the floor. He then turned to the other two. He kicked one in the stomach and hit the other one just about simultaneously with his fist. Both of them went to the floor and didn't move. He looked around at the bodyguard. He was still out cold. He went over to Hammy and began taking off the ropes. Hammy slowly raised his head and, looking at Romo said, "Damn, Mo. Isn't this fun?"

"Can you walk, Hammy?" Romo helped him stand and started toward the door. "Wait a minute, Mo. One of them has my gun." Hammy slowly staggered his way over to the bodyguard and pulled his pistol out of the bodyguard's belt. He then raised his leg and kicked him in the ribs, almost stumbling over on him. Mo grabbed Hammy by the arm to keep him from falling. He put Hammy's arm around his shoulders and neck and walked toward the door that was hanging on one hinge. "Let's get the hell out of here."

"They wanted the tapes, Romo, but I didn't tell them a damn thing."

As they stepped out of the doorway, they looked down the steps. At the bottom of the stairs they saw the man Romo had hit in the throat. He had his hand on a pistol that was in the front of his pants. Romo grabbed his pistol and pulled it out. The man on the stair steps went for his gun. Just about that time, Lieutenant Sparrow and Gene stepped in front of the guy and pushed him backwards. Sparrow stayed at the bottom of the steps while Gene ran up the steps to give Romo a hand with Hammy.

As they left the building, the lieutenant said to Romo, "Follow me. I'll show you the way to the hospital."

"I'm parked right over here," Romo said as he and Gene helped put Hammy in the back seat.

Sparrow turned on the blue light and Romo followed him. In just a few minutes, they were at the hospital. Sparrow had called ahead and had a nurse and a doctor with a gurney waiting when they arrived at the emergency entrance. Hammy was loaded onto the gurney and rolled inside.

Romo, Sparrow and Gene stood out by the car. Romo told the lieutenant that Hammy said the thugs were looking for the tapes. The lieutenant answered, "I haven't had a chance to listen to either one of them yet. Maybe when I get home tonight I can listen to them in peace."

"I hope you were able to get your drugs out of the warehouse in New Jersey, Lieutenant."

"We found the drugs. They were in a false bed in a trailer, thanks to a dope dog that found it. We have loaded it back up, and we're staking out the warehouse, hoping we can make an arrest by daylight. I really thank you, Romo, for that information. It saved a lot of our asses."

About that time, two cars pulled into the emergency room parking area. One man ran inside and came back out in a few minutes with a doctor and two nurses. As they put one man on the gurney, a man standing beside him told the nurse he was having a hard time getting his breath. The doctor put some pressure on his chest and said, "It feels like his sternum is broken. What happened to them?"

The man hesitated for a few minutes, and then finally said, "They were in a car wreck." Two more men were placed on gurneys: one was bleeding from the nose and mouth, and the other one was still knocked out. The nurse was trying to stop the bodyguard's bleeding and the doctor was holding the stethoscope to the other man's chest. He said, "He's breathing, but slowly. Make sure this one gets oxygen as soon as you get him inside."

"Damn, Romo, it's more like a truck hit them," the lieutenant observed.

"Yeah, a tractor trailer truck," Gene said.

"My God, do you think they'll live?" Romo said.

"If you want to go back to North Carolina anytime soon, you had better hope so," Lieutenant Sparrow added. "Do you want to press charges, Romo?"

"I don't, but you might want to ask Hammy."

"Hammy. Is that his name?"

"Yep, that's his real name."

"How in the world did he get that name?" Gene asked.

"He told me his dad said that when he was born, he looked like a small country ham. So they've been calling him Hammy ever since."

"It looks like he's going to be okay," Gene said.

Romo asked, "How did y'all know where to find us, Gene?"

Lieutenant Sparrow spoke up. "After Gene met me at the police department, he told me what happened and handed me the tape recorders. I called your room and didn't get an answer. So, I called the front desk, and the girl said you left the parking deck like a bat out of hell. So, I thought there was only one other place you knew where to go and that would be the Four Jokers. I just figured that's where you were going to see if they had your buddy there."

"Well, I'm glad you showed up when you did. I thought I was going to have to shoot my way out of there."

"Glad it's all turned out okay so far." Lieutenant Sparrow looked at his watch and commented, "It's almost eleven. I've been at this since five this morning. Unless you need us to hang around here, Romo, I think I'm going to take it in. After I get home and sit, I'm going to listen to the tape."

"It's going to tell you all you want to know, Lieutenant."

"I sure hope so, Romo. I'll call you either tonight or early in the morning."

"That will be good, Lieutenant. I'll be waiting for your call."

Twenty-two

Romo went back inside and was standing at the nurse's desk when Hammy and the doctor walked up. Hammy had a large patch on the side of his head. The doctor said, "We wanted Hammy to spend the night so we could keep an eye on him, but he insisted on going home. I believe your buddy is going to be okay. We had to put ten stitches in that gash on the side of his head, but other than a little swelling here and there, he's going to be alright. Keep him up for the next two to three hours just to be sure he doesn't have a concussion."

"Thank you, Doctor. We do appreciate it." They checked out and Romo headed to the hotel.

On the way back, Hammy said, "I think when we get back to the room, I'm going to have me a double and go the hell to bed."

"You heard the doctor when he said you need to stay up for two to three hours just in case you have a concussion. He said somebody had to keep an eye on you."

"Well, you can watch me while I sleep, Romo."

Romo couldn't help but laugh. "Oh, by the way, Lieutenant Sparrow wanted to know if you want to press charges."

"No, we don't need to do that. If I did, all of us would go to jail."

"Yep, I guess you're right."

Romo opened the door to the room and walked in. Hammy stopped, looked around and said, "Damn. Did we do all this?"

"It looks like you put up one hell of a fight."

"I thought I was doing pretty good, and then all of a sudden the lights went out. When I woke up I was tied up in that chair. They wanted those tape recorders, but thank God, you took both of them when you left."

"Sparrow has both of them right now. He hasn't had a chance to listen to them yet. He said he was going to do that when he got home tonight. He left the hospital and went home about an hour ago."

"So he hasn't listened to them yet?"

"No, but he said he would probably be calling here in about an hour or first thing in the morning." Hammy was fixing himself a drink while Romo busied himself placing the television back on the stand and putting the lamps back on the end tables. He set all the chairs upright and placed them under the round table. Hammy sat with both drinks in hand. After handing Romo one, he held his drink in the air and made a toast. "Here's to good partners." Romo touched his glass and responded, "You can say that again."

After finishing their drinks and discussing the day's events, it was almost one o'clock. Hammy stood. "I think I'll go to bed, Mo. I'm a little tired."

"Go ahead, Hammy. I'm going in a few minutes myself. I'm tired, too. It's been one hell of a day." Romo decided to take a shower, thinking it might help him rest a little better. After a hot shower, he pulled down the covers and thought how good that bed was going to feel. It was one-fifteen and he was tired. He was lying on top of the covers when the phone rang. Romo sat straight up and grabbed the phone. "Hello, hello. Yes, this is Romo." He didn't recognize the voice of the caller.

"Romo, this is Lieutenant Sparrow."

"Who?"

"Lieutenant Sparrow. Are you awake?"

"I am now. What time is it?"

"It's three-fifteen. I haven't slept a damn bit. I listened to those tapes, and I'm so fired up, I can't sleep. I need to talk to you bad. Can I come over?"

"Yes," Romo answered. "Come on over. Room ten-oh-four, top floor."

"I'll be there in about thirty minutes."

"Fine. I'll put on a pot of coffee."

"Great. See you shortly."

Mo got up and started the coffee, then went to the bathroom to wash his face with cold water. He still felt like he was half asleep. He went back to check on the coffee. It had just finished brewing. He grabbed a Styrofoam cup and poured himself a cup. He was about to pull out a chair from the round table and sit when Lieutenant Sparrow knocked on the door.

"Damn, Lieutenant, you look rough."

"Yes, I'm sure I do. I need a shave, a bath, and some clean clothes, but I didn't take the time to do that. I had to talk to you."

Romo handed his guest a cup of coffee, and they both sat at the table. Sparrow looked Romo straight in the eyes and said, "We've got a problem, Romo."

"What is it?"

"Where's Hammy?"

"He's in the next room. He went right to sleep as soon as he got in. Talk to me, Lieutenant."

"I truly believe Eddie has been on the take from Zanetti, and most likely, he's the one who killed Paul. But the problem I've got is a tape recording you obtained through some type of torture to get Zanetti to talk. As you know, some people will say anything or say what you want to hear depending on what method you're using to torture them. As you know I can't use this tape. If I do, you and your buddy might go to jail. Also the tape will be inadmissible in court. I've thought and thought about it. We have got to come up with a way to get Eddie to talk. We have the same problem with Tyler's wife; we can't use it against her either. Do you think Tyler knew she was making copies of his keys?"

"I don't think so, Lieutenant. Tyler just told me that she had been acting awful strange lately. He said they were not getting along at all."

"Do you have any ideas about how we might handle this problem?"

"Let me think about it for a few minutes, Lieutenant. We'll come up with something," he said as he got up and poured himself another cup of coffee.

"By the way, nobody has seen Zanetti since yesterday morning. What did you tell him?"

"I just told him that we were taping everything he was telling us and, as soon as I left, I was going to mail it to the John Gotti family in New York. I told him the way I had it figured, he had about two days to get his wife or girlfriend and get the hell as far away from Philadelphia as he could."

"It looks like he took your advice," he said with a grin, "because he can't be found."

"Well good. Maybe, I have helped you guys in that way by getting his ass out of Philadelphia."

"Do you think you could approach Eddie with just hearsay evidence and make him think you have enough solid evidence to get him to crack?"

"I thought about that, but I've only got one shot at it, and if he were to tell me to prove it, I'm screwed." Romo sat staring down at his coffee cup, thinking. All of a sudden he jumped up from the table, almost knocking his coffee over, and said excitedly, "Hold on a minute, Lieutenant. I might have something for you." He ran to the closet and pulled out his suitcase and started digging down to the bottom of it. He found the envelope with the gold Cross pen in it. Holding the envelope up, he walked to the table, sat, and opened it. He emptied the contents of the envelope in front of the lieutenant without touching what was inside.

"It's a gold Cross pen."

Lieutenant Sparrow looked at it and reached for it. Romo grabbed his hand and said, "Hold on, Lieutenant. Let me tell you where I got the pen. As you can see, it's a pen just like most ranked police officers use. When I was going through Paul's truck, I opened the glove box, and I could tell somebody had already been in it. As I was looking at the floorboard, I saw this pen lying there. It was just about under the front seat. If I hadn't been looking I wouldn't have seen it. I think whoever was ransacking Paul's house was looking for his notepad, the one he made all of his notes in. When they were going through his truck trying to find it, they dropped this pen out of their pocket and didn't know it. Do you think Eddie would have a pen like this?"

"Well, he is a sergeant, and most of the guys with that rank do use those gold Cross pens."

"I am pretty sure it was not Paul's; he only used a lead pencil with an eraser. As you know, he was from the old school."

"He was at that. He always listened to what everybody else had to say and kept his own mouth shut."

"I'll tell you what you can do, Lieutenant. Go back to the office and pull Eddie's ticket books. This pen is a black fine point. Check and see what he was using on the day of the murder, and then check and see if he was using the same type of pen the next day. If there is a difference, you can rest assured it's his pen. You might be able to get a fingerprint off this one."

"I think I'll be able to get this done in the office. I can just pull his employee file, which will have his fingerprints on it then get the lab to take the fingerprints off this pen, and we can compare them."

"If you can get that done and it all checks out, you will have a good reason to pull him in," Romo said as he rolled the pen back in the envelope and handed it across the table to Sparrow.

"Man, I'm glad I came over, and we talked about this. I think I have something now that I can work with. I'm going home, take a shower and clean up. I think I can be back at the office by seven-thirty or eight. You go back to bed. I'll call you later in the morning, hopefully by noon, and give you a rundown on what's happening."

Twenty-three

About ten o'clock, there was a light peck on Romo's inside door.

"Come on in, Hammy." Romo had grabbed a pillow and was lying on the sofa. When Hammy walked in, Romo raised up off the sofa and looked at him. "My Lord, Hammy, from the way you look, maybe I should take you back to the hospital." The right side of his face was as purple as an outer layer of an onion with a gold tint surrounding it. His right eye was partially closed. What you could see of the white part of his eyeball was totally red. The right side of his bottom lip was bruised and swollen to the size of a golf ball. "Are you okay?"

"I feel better than I did last night. The only problem I'm having this morning is this hot coffee cup against my lip. Were you able to get some sleep?"

"Not much. Lieutenant Sparrow called me about three-fifteen and needed to talk. He said he couldn't sleep after listening to the tapes so he came over and stayed from about four until five-thirty." As he and Hammy sipped coffee, Romo explained the situation with the tapes and the thoughts the lieutenant had about the gold Cross pen which Romo had found in Paul's truck. He told Hammy the lieutenant felt that with that pen, they might have enough evidence to call Eddie in without having to use the tapes.

"Lieutenant Sparrow thinks he can get Eddie to start talking or confess. He's supposed to call me back here as soon as he finds something, possibly before noon."

Hammy looked at his watch. "It's ten-thirty now. We haven't got long to wait."

"You want to order breakfast or lunch?" Romo asked.

"Either one is fine with me. I'm hungry."

Lunch arrived about eleven-fifteen. Hammy was a slow eater even though he only ordered applesauce, creamy potatoes, and meatloaf. That's about all he could eat because his jaw was swollen, and it still hurt. Hammy was about to finish up when the phone rang.

Anxiously, Romo picked up the phone. "This is Romo." He listened for a minute, and said, "Okay. We'll see you then.

"That was the lieutenant. He said we had a lot to talk about but didn't want to do it over the phone. He said he would be here in about thirty minutes."

"Good. I need to thank him for saving our asses last night."

"They sure did. I'm glad they showed up when they did, or we would have had to shoot our way out of there."

It wasn't long before there was a light knock on the door. Romo answered it and greeted the lieutenant. "I must say,

Lieutenant, you look a damn sight better than you did this morning at four o'clock."

"A hot shower, clean clothes, and a close shave will always put you on the right track."

"I haven't had that yet, Lieutenant, but I'm going to before the day is out."

Hammy stood, walked over and shook Sparrow's hand. "I just want to thank you for saving our asses last night."

"You're welcome, Hammy, and I would like to thank you guys for all you've contributed to the investigation of this case, whether it was done the right way or the wrong way."

"Sit over here, Lieutenant," Romo directed as he started taking away the dirty plates they had left on the table. "We just had lunch. You'll have to excuse this mess."

"At least you've had time to eat. When I leave here, that's going to be my next stop. Well, boys, it's been one hell of a morning. As soon as I got to the station this morning, I turned that pen over to the crime lab and started running the fingerprints on it. Needless to say, Romo, Eddie's fingerprints were all over that pen. We got a good thumb print and an index fingerprint. We also pulled his citation booklet, and you were right. The ink was black on the day of the murder, and the next day it went to a light gray...two different pens altogether. At that point, I called in my captain, John Wiley. He has been on the force for twenty-five years and, for the last fifteen, he has been in homicide. He was real close friends with Paul, and every day since Paul was murdered, he would always ask for an update. Unfortunately, I didn't have anything to tell him until this morning. He was really pleased with the evidence I had, then he really got upset when I told him who I thought it was. His face went white, Romo, then it got blood red. He was mad as hell. He picked up the phone and called the dispatcher and told him to notify Eddie Reynolds to come to his office first thing before he went out on patrol.

"The captain and I were sitting in his office talking when Eddie walked in. The captain didn't say a word. He just pointed at a chair and motioned for him to sit down. I looked at Eddie's shirt pocket. He had two pens: one was a Cross; the other looked like a cheap Bic.

"I asked him, 'Where is your other Cross pen?'"

"'I don't know. I lost it somewhere,' he replied."

I took the pen Romo gave me and laid it on the captain's desk. "Is this it?" I asked.

"He looked at the pen and then looked at me. He answered, 'I don't know if it's mine or not.'"

"It's yours, Eddie. Do you know how I know it's yours?" He shook his head. "Because your fingerprints are on it. That's how I know."

He looked surprised. Then I said to him, "Do you know where we found it, Eddie?" Again, not saying a word, he just shook his head. "It was on the floorboard of Paul Riggs' truck. Why do you think it was on the floorboard of that truck, Eddie?" His face turned red again, but he didn't say a word. "That's another reason I know it was yours. You had used it on the day of Paul's murder, and then you used another pen the next day to write your citations. So, this pen puts you at the scene of the crime. Is there anything you want to say, Eddie? Did you kill Paul Riggs?" He just sat and stared at us as if he couldn't believe what was happening.

"I told him we knew he was the one who stole the gun from of the confiscation room and swapped it for the gun that caused the case to be thrown out of court on the murder charges against one of Zanetti boys. I told him how that really pissed Paul off because he knew it was Paul's case, and how determined Paul was to find out how that gun got out of the warehouse. I told Eddie how close Paul was to finding out who it was, and that's why I, personally, thought that's why he killed Paul.

"I let him that know we were aware he was the one who took the cocaine out of our warehouse and took it to Jersey City. He just dropped his head. It just about took the wind out of him when I told him that. Now, I said, I want you to tell me how Sarah Riggs was involved in all this."

"Again, he just sat there with his head down and never said a word. The captain couldn't take it anymore. He jumped up and walked around his desk and took the police shield off Eddie's shirt. Not giving Eddie a chance to take his gun out of his holster, the captain unsnapped the buckle and took it off himself as he read him his rights. The captain reached down and grabbed Eddie by the front of his shirt and pulled him up and out of the chair. The captain got right in his face, and with clenched teeth advised him, 'You're under arrest for the murder of Paul Riggs, Eddie.' He then handcuffed him with Eddie's own handcuffs. The captain was livid. I had to step in to assist him in taking Eddie downstairs to be locked up. After we booked him, it seemed like no time at all when in came his wife and a lawyer. She signed the bond, and they left. I was told by some of the fellows who were standing outside they could hear his wife cussing him out as they pulled out of the parking lot.

"Needless to say, Tyler was pretty upset as well. I went ahead and told him to take the rest of the day off. When Maria and Eddie left, I asked Gene to follow them home to be sure Eddie didn't leave town. When I left to come over here, Gene was right behind them. So, that is my update as of now. The next thing I need to figure out is how I'm going to get Sarah. I hate this, because of Tyler. He was still at the office when I left, so I have a couple of options. I need to think about it before I go get her in the morning while Tyler is there. He could be of some help if she goes crazy on us. That's my thinking, Romo. If you come up with any better ideas, just let me know." The lieutenant looked at his watch. "It's hard to believe I've been here nearly two hours. I'll call you before I make a move on Sarah."

"Thank you, Lieutenant. I would appreciate that just in case I need to be with Tyler when that happens."

"I understand, Romo." As the lieutenant started out the door, he got a call on his walkie-talkie from Gene, who sounded frantic. "Lieutenant! Lieutenant!" Holding the walkie-talkie up to his mouth, he hesitated at the door and said, "Go ahead, Gene."

"You need to get over here at Eddie's house. He just put a pistol in his mouth and blew the top of his head off. His wife is running around in the front yard throwing her arms up in the air, screaming and going crazy. I could use some help."

"I'm on my way." The lieutenant said to Romo, "I could use some help with this. You want to go?" Romo turned to Hammy.

"Y'all go ahead," Hammy replied to Romo's questioning look. "I'm going to lie down on the couch and rest my head."

Romo and the lieutenant ran out the door. They raced through Philadelphia with a blue light on the dashboard. Cars in front of them pulled to the side, shortening the travel time to their destination. Neighbors had come over and were trying to aid Maria. She was still screaming and hollering. Romo and the lieutenant went inside the house and walked into the den. There sat Eddie in a recliner with his head pointed downward, still in his uniform. There was an exposed hole in the top of his head as big as a tennis ball. There was blood and bone matter stuck to the wall behind him. Some of it had stuck to the ceiling. In his shirt pocket was a white envelope with the letters LT Sparrow hand printed on the top edge. The lieutenant removed the envelope and stuck it in his back pocket.

Looking at Gene, he asked, "Has everybody been called?"

"Yes, sir. I've called the homicide investigators, the coroner, and the ambulance."

"That's good. Thank you, Gene." The lieutenant got Romo's attention and motioned for him to step outside with him. They saw that Maria had quieted down some and was sitting down in the yard. Three or four of her neighbors were consoling her.

"Come on, Romo. Let's go sit in the car and find out what's in this envelope. I'm sure it's a confession letter."

After getting in the car, the lieutenant pulled out the envelope. Inside was a folded letter. On about half of the page was a note handwritten and signed by Eddie. He read it out loud to Romo.

Lieutenant Sparrow, I am writing you this to make a clear confession of the death of Paul Riggs and my involvement. On the afternoon of his murder, I was on patrol. I received a phone call from Sarah Riggs about five-fifteen. She asked if I would meet her at Paul's house within the next fifteen minutes. It just so happened I was free to meet her, and I drove to Paul's townhouse. When I got there, she was sitting in the driveway. I pulled up behind her car and parked my motorcycle. She got out of her car and started walking up the steps to Paul's home without saying a word. I had no idea why she wanted me there until we got inside. Paul opened the door, welcomed us, and invited us in. We went into the kitchen, and Paul asked if we would like to have a drink. I told him I would because I was off duty and was going home from there. Paul turned around and opened the refrigerator door. He was getting the ice out for the drinks when suddenly....

Lieutenant Sparrow stopped reading and, with wide open eyes and tightly closed lips, he looked over at Romo. Romo looked at him anxiously and prompted him, "Go ahead, Lieutenant, read it."

"I think this may hurt."

Twenty-four

The lieutenant glanced back down at the sheet of paper, gesturing as if he couldn't believe what was written. He took a quick look at Romo, then continued reading.

Sarah reached in her pocketbook and pulled out a small pistol. She put it close to the back of Paul's head and pulled the trigger. Paul fell to the floor. I asked her why in the hell she did that. She said Paul was getting too close to finding out how the keys had been made for Zanetti, and she felt like she had no alternative but to do what she did. She needed to find Paul's notepad where he had written down all his information. She started going through drawers and cabinets looking for Paul's notebook. We searched the house over and did not find it. Yes, I searched his truck, and that's where you found my ink pen. I tried to make it look like it had been a break-in. I jerked on the front door from the inside until the framing split, giving the impression it had been a break-in.

I may not be the man you thought I was, but there's one thing I am not. I am not a murderer. I did not kill Paul Riggs. Sarah killed Paul Riggs. This is my dying confession, and it is the truth, so help me God.

Eddie Reynolds

Sparrow looked at Romo, wondering what his reaction to the letter would be. Romo sat quietly, slowly stroking his mustache with his thumb and index finger. Sparrow could tell he was having a hard time digesting what he had just heard.

Finally, Romo said, "This has hit me like a ton of bricks. I'm just wondering how Tyler will take the news."

"I don't know, but we're going to go now and get the bitch," the lieutenant said angrily as he backed out of the drive, spun around and headed out of the development. "I don't know if she's working or not, but we'll go to the house first. It's three-forty-five. I'm sure Tyler will be there by now. What bothers me is that if it was such a shock to Tyler when he thought it was Eddie who killed Paul, how in the hell is he going to feel when he finds out it was his wife who killed him?"

"I have no idea what he's going to do. All I know is I'll be there for him if he needs me."

As they pulled into Tyler's driveway, the lieutenant grabbed the envelope and put the letter back inside his back pocket. "I think I'm going to just let him read the letter and see what happens after that."

"Whatever you think, Lieutenant. I'll be here."

They rang the doorbell and Tyler came to the door. He seemed a little surprised to see Lieutenant Sparrow and

Romo together. "Come on in." He shook the lieutenant's hand and put both of his hands on Romo's shoulder. "I'm glad you came, Uncle Romo." As they walked in, the lieutenant asked Tyler if they could sit at the kitchen table. "There are some things we have to discuss with you."

"Sure, come on back here. Can I fix you guys a drink or a cup of coffee?" They declined the offer. Romo and the lieutenant took a seat, and Tyler sat between them with his hands clasped. After a moment, he asked, "So what's up, fellows?"

Sparrow asked if he had spoken with his mother. "Yes. She told me what happened. I think it was probably best for him to go out that way."

The lieutenant continued. "There was an envelope in Eddie's shirt pocket that had my name on it." He reached into his back pocket, pulled out the envelope and handed it to Tyler. Tyler slowly unfolded it, all the while looking at the lieutenant and Romo. He started reading. You could tell when he got to the part where Eddie said Sarah had pulled a pistol and shot Paul in the back of the head. He sat back in his chair as if he were wondering what he would read next. He cleared his throat and continued reading as tears spilled from his eyes and rolled down his cheek. After he finished, he slowly folded it back up and handed it back to Lieutenant Sparrow.

"I know she has a hell of a temper, and we weren't getting along at all. For some reason it doesn't surprise me that she did this. She can be that hard core. As I think back, she would ask me to go to the store to pick up a gallon of milk when we already had a half a gallon in the refrigerator. Now, I know what she was doing while I was gone; she was making a copy of my key. I never could make her happy. She wanted more than I could provide. She went out and bought that new car we couldn't afford. I told her not to get it, but she bought it anyway."

"What kind of car was it, Tyler?" the lieutenant asked.

"It was a red Audi convertible, and she loves that car although we can't afford it."

"Where is she now?" Sparrow asked. Tyler said she had left a voicemail on the phone saying she was going to work overtime and she would be late getting home. He asked, "Do you think you could get her on the phone?"

Tyler dialed the number of the Stanley and Stanley law firm and asked for Sarah Riggs, only to be told that she had left at lunch and said she was taking the rest of the day off. When Tyler told Sparrow and Romo, the lieutenant asked Romo, "Do you think she's hauled ass, Romo?"

"Yes, I think that's exactly what she did as soon as she found out about Eddie's arrest. She was probably pretty sure he was going to spill the beans."

"Any idea where she'd go?" Sparrow asked Tyler.

"Knowing her, she would head for Canada."

"Why Canada?"

"Because Canada is where she's from originally. I believe the only reason she married me was so she could stay here in the United States. I found out later that she was going to be deported back to Canada sixty days before I married her. I had to fill out a bunch of papers for her to be able to stay here. I had to show the marriage certificate to prove we were married."

Sparrow hesitated for a few moments, then asked, "Do you have a picture of her that we could borrow?"

"Sure. Hold on a minute. There's one in the bedroom." Tyler returned with an eight by ten framed color picture of Sarah. "That's perfect," the lieutenant said as he slid the back off the frame and took out the picture.

"You want to stay here, Romo? I'm going to headquarters and have her picture sent to the airports, train stations, and the border guards in Canada so they can be on the lookout for her."

Tyler interrupted. "I feel sure, Lieutenant, that she drove her car."

"Okay. If she's driving and left at twelve o'clock, she's got a five hour head start to Canada, which is about five hundred miles. That's approximately a six and a half to a seven-hour drive. I'm going to the station and get this picture sent out. Now, I know why we couldn't find anything on her in the U.S. As soon as I get back, I am going to have her checked out in Canada to see if she has a record there. I will be back, hopefully in two or three hours." He got up from the table hastily and started out the door. He stopped, turned around, and spoke to Tyler. "I am so sorry you're having to go through this. There's nothing you could have done to keep any of this from happening." Tyler nodded his head and remained silent.

After the lieutenant left, Romo asked, "Would you like me to fix you a drink, Tyler? I sure could use one."

"Let me fix it, Uncle Romo. I know where everything is." He stood and started opening cabinet doors, taking out glasses and a bottle of Jack Daniels. "Would you like water or something else with it, Uncle Romo?"

"A little Coke if you have it."

Tyler got a can of Coke, the bottle of Jack Daniels, two glasses of ice, and set them all on the table. "Help yourself."

"I know this is hard on you, Tyler, but I think it's better to find out now than later," Romo advised.

"Uncle Romo, Sarah and I really didn't have a marriage. She slept in another bedroom most of the time. A lot of times she would come home from work and go straight to her bedroom and not come out until the next morning. In the last three to four weeks, she has really been acting strange. I got to the point where I just ignored it and did the best I could with the situation."

"Would you like to go over and see your mother?"

"Not really. The way I feel now, I don't think I would be any good to her or anyone else. I believe I want to just sit here for a while. I'll go over and see Mama later tonight." They sat and made casual conversation and had a couple more mixed drinks. The doorbell rang, and Romo wondered who it could be.

Tyler opened the door and found Lieutenant Sparrow holding a brown envelope. Tyler stepped aside and asked him to come in. The lieutenant walked back toward the kitchen. He noticed Romo was having a mixed drink and said, "Do you guys care if I join you? I think I need a drink." He laid the envelope on the table and while fixing himself a drink, he brought them up to date.

"Fellows, you're not going to believe all I've found out about Sarah." He took a sip of his drink and began taking the papers out of the envelope. "To start with, Tyler, she's not twenty-three years old; she's thirty-two. This woman is totally a gangster." He started reading from a sheet of paper. "When she was eighteen, she went to work for a small clothing company. After three months, she had embezzled about three thousand dollars before they caught up with her. At nineteen, she was charged with writing bad checks. At that same age, she got into a fight at a nightclub and cut another woman with a knife. She declared it was self-defense and was placed on probation.

"When she was twenty, she and her older brother were arrested for robbing a jewelry store in Ontario. Her brother got ten years in prison because he was the one that had the gun. She got five years, but she only pulled two years of it. She got out for good behavior." He slid one sheet of paper off of the stack.

"A couple of months later, two exclusive homes down by a lake were broken into. Ten thousand dollars was taken from one house and jewelry valued at twenty thousand was taken from the other one. The last house broken into had an outside video camera set up which revealed the robber was someone small in stature. It was rather obvious it was a woman. Investigators were pretty sure it was Sarah, but they were unable to get the evidence to make a charge. Shortly after that, she ended up in Philadelphia and went to work for the law practice here in Philly as a paralegal.

"Within a year after she arrived here, she had a new birth certificate, driver's license and social security number. She had a certificate from a community college in Philadelphia where she graduated after taking a two-year course in criminal justice. Her real name is Jennifer Haskell. After getting her new driver's license and birth certificate, she was able to change her name to Sarah Ames. I think she learned how to do a lot of forgery from being in a woman's prison, and as a paralegal, she learned the ins and outs quickly. Her visa only had two months left before she had to go back to Canada. It was just her luck to have married you, Tyler, in that period of time. That's the only reason she was not extradited to Canada.

"When I talked to the detectives in Canada earlier, they said a homicide detective by the name of Paul Riggs had requested the same information about three or four weeks ago, and they had faxed it to him. After sending that info to Paul, the Canadian detectives went over and visited Sarah's mother, I mean Jennifer's mother, and told her that a homicide detective was inquiring about her daughter. I think they were thinking if they gave her this information, and she talked to her daughter about it, it might scare her into coming back to Canada. They wanted the opportunity to talk to her about the two break-ins."

Twenty-five

"Now let me tell you what I think happened. When her mother called her and told her about Paul checking out her background and obtaining information concerning her past, that's when she made up her mind to take him out. She knew that once he was told, it wouldn't be long before he would put the pieces together. I thought it might have been Zanetti who ordered the hit, but now I don't think so. She was running scared of what Paul was going to do. She knew her time was fast running out, and something had to be done quickly. She had to take Paul out, find all his notes, and, hopefully, find the information the Canadian detectives had sent him about her background. She wanted to be sure she wasn't implicated in any way and wanted to keep anyone from knowing about her background."

Tyler spoke up. "That's why the last two weeks, Dad didn't come over to visit like he used to, and he didn't have much to say when I went over there. I knew something was wrong. He knew all along who Sarah was and was afraid to tell me or didn't want to until he had the evidence to prove it."

Lieutenant Sparrow said, "I never found Paul's copy of the information that was faxed to him from Canada. I think maybe he might have destroyed it to keep anybody else from finding it until he could put it all together."

Romo added, "That's the way Paul did things. You know, Lieutenant, that Paul would keep everything to himself until he could put all the pieces together."

"I left word for the detectives up there to call me on my cell phone as soon as they heard something about Sarah. I'm almost sure she was going to drive to Canada." The lieutenant observed the time. "It's been over three hours since the word went out to the border guards. I'm hoping to hear something before it gets too late. It's about a seven hour drive so she has had time to get to the border. Maybe we'll hear something pretty soon. At least I hope so.

~ * ~

"Well, boys, it's eleven o'clock and we've drunk three-fourths of a fifth of Jack. Evidently, something has gone wrong or else they would have her by now. So I'm thinking, Romo, we need to take you back to the hotel. As soon as I hear something, I'll call you or come by your room tomorrow morning."

"That's fine with me, Lieutenant. It's getting late."

"Would you like to come back to the hotel with me and spend the night? At least you won't be here alone," Romo asked Tyler.

"That's okay, Uncle Romo. I think I'm going to drive over to Mom's house. I have a feeling I'll be up with her all night. I need to tell her Eddie didn't shoot Dad, and that it was Sarah."

"How do you feel, Tyler?"

"It all seems like a dream to me. To Sarah, I was just a convenience. It was only a matter of time before she would have been taken back to Canada, anyway. I feel like I was an idiot all along, and I'm mad at myself for being so stupid."

"We'd better go, Romo," the lieutenant advised. "It's ten after eleven already, and I've got to be up early in the morning and start filling out reports. Damn, what a report this is going be."

Tyler walked out out with them and locked up. He added, "Just need to go to Mom's now and see if I can calm her down."

"I've got a feeling you've got a big job on your hands, buddy," Romo said. "I'll call you tomorrow. I'm planning on leaving early Sunday morning, and I'd like to see you before I leave."

"That would be good, Uncle Romo. Call or come by anytime."

On the way back to the hotel, Romo asked Sparrow, "Do you think it's possible she might have stopped and got a motel room, Lieutenant?"

"That's a possibility, but I think her number one priority is to get back into Canada. She has friends there that will help keep her out of sight. But I think we'll know a lot more by morning. I heard you say that you're going to be leaving and going back to North Carolina Sunday morning?"

"That's the plan, if all goes well," Romo answered as they pulled up in front of the hotel.

"I'll call you in the morning, Romo, or I'll come over, depending on what information I have."

"I would appreciate that, Lieutenant. You have a good night."

Although Hammy's door was closed, Romo could hear him snoring. As he got ready for bed, Romo could not help but think about Tyler and what he must be going through. He didn't think, however, that Tyler seemed to take it too hard about Sarah. He thought Tyler was angrier at himself than anything else.

The next morning Romo was up early. He was sitting at the little table staring out over the city when he heard Hammy knocking on the door.

"Come on in, Hammy. I must say you're looking better this morning."

"I feel better too. My head is still a little sore, but, other than that, I feel fine."

After taking about an hour to discuss the latest events concerning Sarah and her whereabouts, Hammy declared, "Damn. That girl is just an outlaw and murderer, isn't she? I know Tyler is going through a hard time about now."

"I thought I would go over after a while and see how he's doing," Romo said. "I'll probably need you to follow me back to the car rental place and drop the car off. We'll leave early Sunday morning to go back home."

"That sounds good to me. I think raising pigs is a lot easier than this, but it's not half as much fun!"

Romo looked at him, smiling, showing those deep dimples in his cheeks. "We've had one hell of a week. Can't say I would like doing this again." Romo had hardly gotten the words out of his mouth when the phone rang. "Romo, this is Lieutenant Sparrow. I just left Tyler's home. His mother spent the night at his house, so I had a chance to discuss the situation with both of them. Tyler seems to be taking everything pretty well, but his mother has enough

Xanax in her to kill a horse. Other than that, she seems to be doing fine. I've got an update on Sarah's situation. They called me early this morning and gave me a rundown. I've got Gene with me, and we'd like to come over and share that update with you. We also want to wish you well on your way home. We can be there in about fifteen minutes if that's alright with you."

Hammy and Romo were drinking their second cup of coffee when the lieutenant and Gene knocked on the door. Romo opened the door and greeted them with a handshake. "Good morning, guys. Go over and have a seat at the table. Would y'all like a cup of coffee?"

"No thanks. We don't have a lot of time. We have to get back to the office."

The lieutenant opened the discussion. "They had a hell of a time at the Canadian border last night."

"What happened?"

"I'll explain it to you like they explained it to me. They told me that when Sarah pulled up at the border booth, the guard looked at her passport and recognized her. He made her pull over to the side of the road and asked her to turn off her engine. When he said that, she took off like a bat out of hell, spinning the tires until they were smoking. Two officers pursued her. They said she started into a long curve and ran off the right shoulder of the road. She over-corrected and, when the car hit the pavement, she was sideways. The car started flipping in the middle of the road. Every time it flipped and came down and hit the road, it was like it exploded. Parts were flying everywhere. After about three or four flips, it stopped, and slid off down the left side of an embankment.

"They said she was bad off. They had to call a helicopter in to transport her to the hospital. When they searched the car, they found a twenty-five automatic in the glove box. They're going to send it to us so we can check out the ballistics. I'm sure it's the gun that killed Paul. As of this morning, they have her hooked up to a breathing machine. She has a broken back, serious spinal cord injury, and several broken ribs. They think that, if she pulls through, she'll be paralyzed from the neck down, so it looks like she's in pretty bad shape. I doubt she'll ever be able to stand trial in Canada, much less the United States."

Romo sat, shaking his head. Then, he said, "Well, if she does live, being paralyzed from the neck down for the rest your life is punishment enough for anyone. I hate it for her, but you know the old saying, 'What goes around comes around.'"

"I agree with you. To be so young and be paralyzed for the rest of her life is punishment enough. Now, Romo, we have to get back. You know the drill... nothing is finished until the paperwork is done."

"Yep, I understand that, Lieutenant."

"Hammy, it was nice meeting you," Sparrow said, "and I want to thank you, personally, for all your assistance in closing this case."

"You're more than welcome, Lieutenant. Glad I could be of some help."

As Romo walked Gene and the lieutenant to the door, he turned to Gene, and said, "Thanks, Gene, for all your help. If it had not been for you taking those tapes to the lieutenant, and you guys following up, I'm sure Hammy and I would be in one hell of a mess by now. So, thanks to all of you."

With a firm handshake, the lieutenant said, "If you're ever back in Philly, look us up. We'll go out and have a beer." He looked over at Hammy who was sitting at the table and added, "And be sure you bring Hammy along."

"I couldn't leave him behind, Lieutenant. He is the best partner I've ever had."

"I believe that," Sparrow said with a grin. "You guys have a safe trip back. Hope to see you again under different circumstances, Romo."

"Same here. You guys have a good day."

As Romo closed the door, he stopped and took a deep breath. Looking over at Hammy, he confessed, "I'm so glad all of this is over, and we can get back to North Carolina. I think I need to ride over, and see Tyler and his mother, just to see if there's anything I can do to help them. After that, I need to see a friend of mine who lives beside Paul's place. Then I'd like to go by the orphan home, and to the place where we scattered Paul's ashes, and pay my respect to Paul. Do you want to go or just hang around and rest?"

"If you don't mind, Romo, I think I'll order myself some lunch, watch a little television, and rest."

"Okay. It might be late this afternoon before I get back."

"That's fine. Take your time."

"When I get back, I'll get you to follow me to return the rental car if you feel up to it."

"You got it, buddy. Be careful. See you after a while."

Twenty-six

When Romo pulled up in Tyler's driveway, he didn't know what to expect. He knew there was not a whole lot he could say, other than extending his sympathy.

"Come on in, Uncle Romo," Tyler greeted him. He called out to his mother. "Uncle Romo is here, Mom."

She walked out of the kitchen wiping her hands with a dish towel, put her arms around Romo's neck, and started crying.

"I am so sorry about all of this. I had no idea Eddie and Sarah had all this going on. Lieutenant Sparrow came by early this morning and told us what happened to Sarah and the condition she's in. She played all of us, including Paul."

"Yes, she did, Maria. I just wanted to stop by and see how you guys are doing."

She wiped her tears away with the towel and spoke with a trembling voice. "We're going to be fine, Romo. We have each other, and that's what counts."

"I'm going to be driving back in the morning early," Romo said, "so if there's anything I can do just let me know."

"No, there's nothing. It's something Tyler and I have got to work out on our own."

"I understand, but if you guys need to get away for a while, you can always come to North Carolina."

"Thanks, Uncle Romo," Tyler said. "Don't you be gone for so long. Next time you come, I sure hope it will be under better circumstances."

"I do too, Tyler."

"Would you like to stay for lunch, Romo?" Maria asked.

"No thanks, Maria, and if it's okay with you guys, I will just go on. I've got a couple more stops I'd like to make before going back to the hotel."

Tyler and Maria followed him to the door. "Be careful going back," Maria said. Tyler followed Romo out on the porch and closed the door behind him. "Uncle Romo, thank you so much for coming. The lieutenant said if it hadn't been for you and your partner, they never would have been able to solve this case."

"I didn't do any more than Paul would've done for me, Tyler. I loved my brother."

"I know, and he loved you, too." Tyler put both arms around Romo shoulders and told him, "I love you, too."

"I love you, Tyler. Call me and let me know how you're getting along."

"I will, Uncle Romo, and you be careful going back."

As he pulled out of the driveway, Romo thought about the positive attitude Maria and Tyler had, and he felt they were going to be okay.

As he drove toward Jessie's, he thought it was going to be somewhat of an emotional visit. When he pulled into her driveway and started walking toward her door, without knowing why, he felt nervous.

He rang the doorbell and before it stopped ringing, the door opened. Jessie reached out and hugged him. She put both arms around his neck so quickly he almost fell backwards down the steps. He held her tightly and picked her up. Both her feet were swinging in the air. "Well, this is a nice greeting," he said happily.

He eased her down. She turned around and walked back inside. Romo followed. She set two cups on the bar and started pouring the coffee. She looked at him, occasionally, but didn't say a word. Finally, Romo asked, "Are you okay?"

"Yes, I'm fine. Are you okay?" she said.

"Yes, I'm good."

"I wish you would have called me, occasionally, just to let me know you were alright. From all the news I have been hearing and knowing you were right in the middle of it, I was really worried."

"What did you hear?"

"The first thing was that Van Zanetti had been kidnapped, tortured, and he had confessed to so much he had to leave town. As soon as I heard that, I knew right away you were involved. Then, I heard about three of the Mafia guys who were sent to the hospital in serious condition. Next, I heard about a police officer committing suicide after confessing to murdering Paul. And I knew you were right in the middle of that, too, and it worried me. That's all I've had on my mind for the last few days."

"Damn. News travels fast around here. Did you hear all that on the street?"

"No. I've got friends in high places, big boy. Anything that goes on in this town, I can find out about it. And here you sit...calm, just as though nothing has happened."

"Well, nothing has happened to me."

Jessie stared at him, squinting her eyes, and tightening her lips. "But I didn't know that, damn it, Romo!"

"At the time, I couldn't call. I didn't want to take a chance of getting you involved."

Jessie took a deep breath, a sip of coffee, then said, "I realize you and I are not serious with each other, but damn it, I care about you, and I didn't want to see you get hurt. Is that so hard for you to understand?"

"No, and I care about you. That's why I did what I did. Not seeing you or calling you was to protect you."

"It's sure something I don't want to go through again," she said, emphatically.

"Believe me. It's something I don't want to go through again either. And by the way, that police officer did not murder Paul. Your information was wrong. It was his daughter-in-law, Sarah."

"I can't believe that!" she said, surprised.

He explained the whole scenario to her and filled her in on what had happened up to this morning. She seemed to be shocked. "That's unbelievable," she said.

"You can't put anything past a woman, Jessie."

"And for your best interest, you need to keep that in mind," she answered with a smile as she poured more coffee. "So what's your plan from this point on?"

"When I leave here, I'm going to pay my respects at the children's home where Paul's ashes were spread. Then, I guess I'll go back to the hotel, check on Hammy, and get packed so we can leave early in the morning."

"Oh. So you're going back that soon?"

"I need to get Hammy back home so his personal doctor can follow up on his health."

"I suppose this will be your last visit here?"

"I wouldn't say that," Romo replied with a frown on his face. "I will probably have to come back and check up on you."

"I would hope so. I realize we've only known each other for a short time. And yes, as you probably know, I have grown fond of you. You are the only man I've felt like I have a connection with in a long time."

"I felt the connection, too. You're shown me a lot of things I didn't think were possible. I never thought I could be intimate with a woman again and have feelings for her. You gave me hope. I know now that I can fall in love and maybe get married again. Before I met you, I didn't think that was possible. Thanks to you, I think I can move on and maybe get on with my life."

"I'm confident we have something special. I think if we had more time, we could figure it out. I must tell you how much I've enjoyed my time with you. You're like a breath of fresh air and, just maybe, you can fly up some weekend and spend some time in Philadelphia."

"I think I can do that."

"You have my phone number. Just call. I'll make time for you."

As Romo took his last sip of coffee and stood, Jessie walked over to him and put her arms around his waist. When she looked up at him, Romo reached down and kissed her lightly on the lips. "I'll be back. I can't say exactly when, but I will."

"That will be great. I look forward to seeing you again. Don't make it too long."

As he started down the steps, Jessie called out, "Hey, Romo! Don't be surprised if your doorbell rings one day and when you open it, I'll be standing there."

"I look forward to that."

Romo got back in the car, backed out of the drive, and about a block away, he pulled up to a stop sign. He paused and took a deep breath. *What a woman*, he thought. *She has everything a man would want.*

Romo headed south toward the children's home. When he arrived, he noticed there were only a few cars in the parking lot. He decided to walk down to the ballpark. He didn't tell anyone he was going on the field since he would only be there for few minutes. He walked down the steps and across the infield. He stood in centerfield, gazing around at the neatly cut grass, and he knew this is where Paul would want to be.

As he stood there, thoughts of his childhood started racing through his mind. He remembered the time Paul laid on the floor beside his bed and held his hand because he had awakened from a bad dream. Paul always made sure he was covered up at night in the winter months. Romo would never forget all the little made-up bedtime stories Paul would whisper to him before he went to sleep.

As Romo turned and started to walk away, he stopped suddenly, and turned around gazing over the field. "I hope you are satisfied, Paul, that we caught the person who took your life. I might not have gone about it in the right way, but I hope you'll forgive me for that. You know me, and patience is something I don't have. I love you, Paul. Rest in peace."

Romo started toward the complex. As he got closer, he noticed a man standing with a small woman beside him. It was Father McConnell, smiling and holding out his hand.

Father McConnell said, "Let me introduce you to somebody you may remember." The woman was dressed totally in black. Her hair was completely gray and pulled straight back in a bun. She appeared to be sixty-five or seventy years old. She reached out her hand and introduced herself. "I'm Miss Fraser. It is so good to see you, Romo, Do you remember me?"

"No, ma'am. Can't say that I do."

"I'm the one who looked after you when Paul wasn't around. I'm the only one he would let look after you. He was very protective of you. I have a lot of fond memories of you and Paul. When you saw one, you saw the other. He was always walking around holding your hand...down the hall, in the lunch room line, wherever. He would not let you out of his sight. He really loved you, Romo. The last time I saw Paul was at his father's funeral. He took it pretty hard. Since his mother's heart attack and death two years earlier, Paul had been his dad's caregiver. Mr. and Ms. Riggs sure did love Paul. When he was at Penn State, they would drive up every weekend to see him. They bragged about him all the time. They truly loved him."

"I loved him too," Romo said. "He was a good brother to me."

Ms. Fraser continued, "He wasn't your blood brother, but he loved you as much as if you had been. Sometimes, I think he thought you were his real brother."

Romo's eyes widened, and he turned towards Ms. Fraser as if to correct her. "Hold on a minute. Ms. Fraser, are you trying to tell me that Paul was not my real brother?"

"Well, honey, I thought you knew that."

"Paul was my real brother, wasn't he?" he asked, hoping for reassurance.

Ms. Fraser looked up at Father McConnell as if to say, "I've messed up now." She opened her mouth to speak but it took a few seconds for the words to come out.

"Romo, he was not your blood brother but he was as much a brother to you as a blood brother could be. He loved you so much."

"How can that be?" Romo asked. "I remember him leading me out of the mobile home and sitting me down in the yard away from the fire."

"That can't be so. Paul was here a good week before you arrived."

"I'm telling you, Paul picked me up and carried me out of that house."

"Romo, the investigator said the fire started in the back of the mobile home. They seemed to think your mother was smoking in bed after she had put you down for the night. However, the firemen couldn't figure out how you got out of the house on your own. You were too small and not capable of opening the door, and there was no one else around to help you. When the fire department got there, you were sitting in the front yard holding a small teddy bear. They took you to the hospital. You had no burns; you were fine. They brought you here about two days later. I think Paul was standing at the door when you came in. He grabbed your hand and walked in with you.

"I'll never forget that day when you came walking in holding that little brown teddy bear. We had a hard time getting you to give it up. We finally had to ask Paul to see if he could get it away from you. We had rules in place. Nothing like that was allowed in the bedrooms. The only thing you could have was an extra blanket. Paul was the only one who could get you to give up the teddy bear. He had to promise he would give it back. As time went by, Paul was the only one you would listen to.

"Paul's situation was a pitiful one. He only lived about three or four miles from your house. His house blew up from a faulty gas heating system about two weeks before your house burned. The firemen said that when they went into the house, Paul was lying in the hallway propped up against a bedroom door that was locked from the inside.

"He was overcome with smoke when they carried him outside. They burst in the locked room and found a three-year-old boy. They think it was his baby brother, and that he had tried to get the door open, but because it was locked, he just sat down and was talking to his brother on the other side, but the child passed away from smoke inhalation. Paul was in the hospital for about four or five days before they brought him here. His case was similar to yours. All the paperwork and identification information on who you were, and who he was, all burned in the fire. We ran pictures in the newspaper and did all we could to find a relative for you and him, but no one came forward. So, when there was an opportunity for you to be adopted by a nice family from North Carolina, we decided to let you go. We knew you would be better off. Paul was happy for you, too, although he missed you. He knew you were going to be happy and that made him happy. About eight months later, the Riggs family here in Philadelphia, adopted Paul."

Romo didn't know what to say. He just stood and looked at Ms. Fraser, surprised at what she was telling him.

"He wasn't your blood brother," Mrs. Fraser said. "But let me say this, Romo. You could not have had a blood brother that loved you any more than Paul loved you. You can rest assured that in Paul's heart, you were truly his brother. And I'm sure you felt the same way."

"Thank you, Ms. Fraser, for sharing this with me. It's a little shocking, but I understand how something like that can happen. But to me, Paul will always be my brother, and there's nothing anybody can say or ever will say that will cause me to have a different opinion."

"That's exactly the way you should feel, and I am very proud of both of you boys. You and Paul grew up to be fine men, and I'm honored that I had something to do with that." Romo reached down and gave Ms. Fraser a kiss on the cheek and embraced her affectionately.

As he drove back to the hotel, he ran questions through his mind about the night of the fire and how Paul led him out the door. *Maybe I was overcome by smoke and imagined Paul leading me out. He did live a good distance from my house, and his house had burned two weeks before mine. He was already at the children's home when I was taken there.* Romo decided that most likely what he thought happened couldn't have been so.

He drove into the parking lot at seven-thirty. He needed to return the rental car so he would ask Hammy to follow him. When he got to his room, Hammy walked in and before he could mention the car return, Hammy said, "There's a shoebox over there on the table for you." The box was wrapped in baling twine. It had ROMO printed on the top in big capital letters. Hammy continued, "Tyler brought it by. He said he and his mother were cleaning out the closets and getting rid of all of Sarah's things when he found this box. He said his dad brought it over for him to keep until he found a place to live. This was right after he and his mother had separated. He said he knew we were going back in the morning, so he brought it over this afternoon."

Romo checked out the box. It looked like some kid had printed his name with a red crayon. "What do you think it is, Romo?"

"I have no idea, but we'll find out right now."

The string had been tied in a knot so he had to use his knife to cut it loose. As he opened the box, there lay a little brown teddy bear. "This is Boo Boo, Hammy, the teddy bear I was holding when," Romo hesitated, "when I was taken out of my burning house."

There was a folded piece of paper lying on top of the teddy bear. The paper had turned a dingy yellow from age, so he was careful as he opened it. It was obvious from the print that it had been written by a young child. Romo started reading it aloud.

Romo, here is Boo Boo, the teddy bear you would not let go of the night of the fire.

You held on tight to him down the smoky hallway and out into the yard. It was a cold night. I think Boo Boo helped keep you warm. I told you I would give it back when you let me have it at the children's home, so here it is.

Romo explained, "They wouldn't let me keep it in the orphanage, so I gave it to Paul to keep for me."

Hammy was surprised. "You never told me you were taken out of a fire when you were a child, and I didn't know you were in an orphanage."

"It's a long story, Hammy. I'll explain it all on the way back to North Carolina. Now, let's return the rental car. When we get back, we'll pack up and be ready to leave early in the morning."

On the way back, Romo didn't have much to say. Hammy was obviously feeling better, because he did all the talking. Back at the hotel, they began packing to get ready for their early morning trip. When Hammy had gone to bed, Romo picked up the shoebox. He took Boo Boo out of the box and sat staring at it. He held it with both hands and gazed into its button eyes and began reminiscing about the night of the fire.

Romo remembered standing in the hall, holding Boo Boo and looking at his mother's bedroom door. The hall was filling with smoke, so he could hardly see the door anymore. Paneling in the hallway was beginning to burn. The entire house was ablaze. All of a sudden, he felt two arms wrapped around him, picking him up, and heading down the smoky hallway. When they approached the door, it was open, but there were no steps leading down to the ground. *It was only a short distance, so Paul picked me up and jumped. We rolled on the ground. We got up, and he led me to the edge of the road. I was still holding Boo Boo. The last thing I remember about Paul that night was that he was sitting beside me with his arm around me telling me everything was going to be alright. The next thing I remember, I was sitting in a fire truck with its red lights flashing, and a lot of commotion going on.*

Romo sat and thought and thought. Paul was with him that night, there was no doubt about it. He concluded that not only was Paul his brother, he was also his guardian angel. Romo laid back on the bed and with the teddy bear on his chest, he felt such comfort that he very soon went to sleep.

The next morning he and Hammy were up before daylight, carrying their luggage to the truck. "It looks like it's going to be a fine morning for traveling."

"Yes, it does," Romo replied. "And I'm looking forward to it."

"So am I, buddy," Hammy agreed as they got into the truck.

They pulled out of the hotel parking lot and started toward I-95 south. The sun was a bright orange coming up across the Delaware River, sending an awesome glow over the city skyline. As they drove, Romo looked back at the city that was waking up to a beautiful sunrise and thought, "With all the emotions I've experienced this week, I can truly say this is the City of Brotherly Love."

Meet Mike Axsom

Mike grew up in the small town of Eden, North Carolina. He became a police officer in his hometown, where he served for five years in that capacity.

Seeking a new challenge, he worked as a manager in the textile industry. Later, he transitioned into the sale of textile machinery, traveling extensively in the United States, Canada and Mexico.

After retiring, Mike owned and operated a classic car parts business and a custom framing/art gallery business.

Now retired, Mike loves to spend time with his two granddaughters, Avery and Sydney. He enjoys golfing, shag dancing, reading, and writing books. Mike continues to write and is working on his fourth novel. He currently resides in Greensboro, North Carolina.

Visit Our Website

*For The Full Inventory
Of Quality Books:*

Wings ePress, Inc

*Quality trade paperbacks and downloads
in multiple formats,
in genres ranging from light romantic comedy to general
fiction and horror.
Wings has something for every reader's taste.
Visit the website, then bookmark it.*
We add new titles each month!

*Wings ePress Inc.
3000 N. Rock Road
Newton, KS 67114*

www.ingramcontent.com/pod-product-compliance
Lightning Source LLC
Chambersburg PA
CBHW061033120726
47910CB00006B/2233